Expect the unexpected . . .

"Giovanna!" Elizabeth called, waving. "Here we are!"

Jessica opened her mouth to call out, too, but all that came out was a croak. For once in her life, Jessica was speechless.

Giovanna smiled and walked toward them. She was as tall and elegant as a fashion model. She had beautiful olive skin, clear hazel eyes, and long dark hair that swung around her shoulders. To top it off, she was wearing a black leather jacket that Jessica had fallen in love with when she'd seen it in Image *magazine.*

Jessica swallowed. She could forget about the makeover, and about teaching Giovanna what clothes to wear. Giovanna could probably teach her *a thing or two!*

Bantam Books in the SWEET VALLEY TWINS AND FRIENDS series
Ask your bookseller for the books you have missed

#1 BEST FRIENDS
#2 TEACHER'S PET
#3 THE HAUNTED HOUSE
#4 CHOOSING SIDES
#5 SNEAKING OUT
#6 THE NEW GIRL
#7 THREE'S A CROWD
#8 FIRST PLACE
#9 AGAINST THE RULES
#10 ONE OF THE GANG
#11 BURIED TREASURE
#12 KEEPING SECRETS
#13 STRETCHING THE TRUTH
#14 TUG OF WAR
#15 THE OLDER BOY
#16 SECOND BEST
#17 BOYS AGAINST GIRLS
#18 CENTER OF ATTENTION
#19 THE BULLY
#20 PLAYING HOOKY
#21 LEFT BEHIND
#22 OUT OF PLACE
#23 CLAIM TO FAME
#24 JUMPING TO CONCLUSIONS
#25 STANDING OUT
#26 TAKING CHARGE
#27 TEAMWORK
#28 APRIL FOOL!
#29 JESSICA AND THE BRAT ATTACK
#30 PRINCESS ELIZABETH
#31 JESSICA'S BAD IDEA
#32 JESSICA ON STAGE
#33 ELIZABETH'S NEW HERO
#34 JESSICA, THE ROCK STAR
#35 AMY'S PEN PAL
#36 MARY IS MISSING
#37 THE WAR BETWEEN THE TWINS
#38 LOIS STRIKES BACK
#39 JESSICA AND THE MONEY MIX-UP
#40 DANNY MEANS TROUBLE
#41 THE TWINS GET CAUGHT
#42 JESSICA'S SECRET
#43 ELIZABETH'S FIRST KISS
#44 AMY MOVES IN
#45 LUCY TAKES THE REINS
#46 MADEMOISELLE JESSICA
#47 JESSICA'S NEW LOOK
#48 MANDY MILLER FIGHTS BACK
#49 THE TWINS' LITTLE SISTER
#50 JESSICA AND THE SECRET STAR
#51 ELIZABETH THE IMPOSSIBLE
#52 BOOSTER BOYCOTT
#53 THE SLIME THAT ATE SWEET VALLEY
#54 THE BIG PARTY WEEKEND
#55 BROOKE AND HER ROCK-STAR MOM
#56 THE WAKEFIELDS STRIKE IT RICH
#57 BIG BROTHER'S IN LOVE!
#58 ELIZABETH AND THE ORPHANS
#59 BARNYARD BATTLE
#60 CIAO, SWEET VALLEY!

Sweet Valley Twins and Friends Super Editions
#1 THE CLASS TRIP
#2 HOLIDAY MISCHIEF
#3 THE BIG CAMP SECRET
#4 THE UNICORNS GO HAWAIIAN

Sweet Valley Twins and Friends Super Chiller Editions
#1 THE CHRISTMAS GHOST
#2 THE GHOST IN THE GRAVEYARD
#3 THE CARNIVAL GHOST
#4 THE GHOST IN THE BELL TOWER

SWEET VALLEY TWINS AND FRIENDS

Ciao, Sweet Valley!

Written by
Jamie Suzanne

Created by
FRANCINE PASCAL

A BANTAM SKYLARK BOOK
NEW YORK • TORONTO • LONDON • SYDNEY • AUCKLAND

RL 4, 008–012

CIAO, SWEET VALLEY!

A Bantam Skylark Book / July 1992

Sweet Valley High® and Sweet Valley Twins and Friends are trademarks of Francine Pascal

Conceived by Francine Pascal

Produced by Daniel Weiss Associates, Inc.
33 West 17th Street
New York, NY 10011

Cover art by James Mathewuse

Skylark Books is a registered trademark of Bantam Books, a division of Bantam Doubleday Dell Publishing Group, Inc. Registered in U.S. Patent and Trademark Office and elsewhere.

All rights reserved.
Copyright © 1992 by Francine Pascal.
Cover art copyright © 1992 by Daniel Weiss Associates, Inc.
No part of this book may be reproduced or transmitted in any form or by any means, electronic or mechanical, including photocopying, recording, or by any information storage and retrieval system, without permission in writing from the publisher.
For information address: Bantam Books

If you purchased this book without a cover you should be aware that this book is stolen property. It was reported as "unsold and destroyed" to the publisher and neither the author nor the publisher has received any payment for this "stripped book."

ISBN 0-553-15940-2

Published simultaneously in the United States and Canada

Bantam Books are published by Bantam Books, a division of Bantam Doubleday Dell Publishing Group, Inc. Its trademark, consisting of the words "Bantam Books" and the portrayal of a rooster, is Registered in U.S. Patent and Trademark Office and in other countries. Marca Registrada. Bantam Books, 666 Fifth Avenue, New York, New York 10103.

PRINTED IN THE UNITED STATES OF AMERICA

OPM 0 9 8 7 6 5 4 3 2 1

Ciao, Sweet Valley!

One

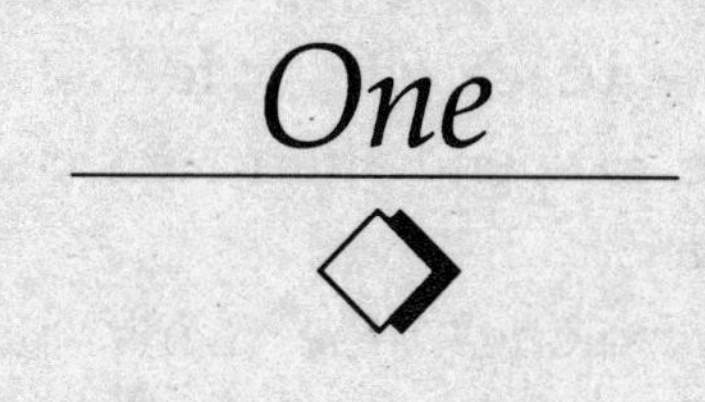

"I've never understood how you can get up so *early* on Saturday morning," Jessica Wakefield said, rubbing her eyes sleepily as she walked into the kitchen. "It's barely dawn."

Elizabeth Wakefield looked up from the stove and smiled at her twin. "It's almost ten, Jessica!" she said, laughing.

"Exactly," Jessica replied with a yawn. "The stores aren't even open yet. I wouldn't be up myself if the Howards' dog hadn't started barking right under my window."

Jessica always found it hard to believe that with their identical long blond hair, blue eyes, and dimples, she and Elizabeth could still be so different. Jessica loved to sleep as late as possible and then get together with her friends in the Unicorn Club, a group of the prettiest and most popular girls at Sweet Valley Middle School.

Elizabeth, on the other hand, liked to get an early start so she could go horseback riding or jogging on the beach with a few of her friends. She also loved to spend afternoons curled up with a good mystery.

"What's cooking?" the twins' older brother, Steven, asked as he came into the kitchen. "I'm so hungry I could eat a cow."

Elizabeth laughed. "Would you settle for pancakes, Steven?"

"If I have to," Steven joked. "Where are Mom and Dad?"

"They went jogging," Elizabeth said. "They said we should go ahead and eat." She filled a platter with pancakes and took them to the table.

As Jessica glanced at the morning mail, her eyes fell on an official-looking envelope addressed to Elizabeth. "What's this?" she asked, picking it up.

"It's the information on GO," Elizabeth said. "I called the number we saw in the newspaper last week and asked them to send it."

"What's GO?" Steven asked.

"It's a foreign student exchange program," Elizabeth explained. "Jess and I saw an article about it in the paper."

Jessica opened the envelope and pulled out some papers. "Wow, Elizabeth!" she said, scanning the pages. "If we're chosen, we get to spend three whole weeks going to school in a foreign country! Paris, here we come!"

Steven sat down and piled some pancakes on his plate. "Really? Three whole weeks?" he asked.

"Yep," Jessica said dreamily. "Think of the fantastic shopping we could do in Paris, Lizzie!"

"Shopping in Paris?" Steven said, laughing. "On *your* allowance?"

Jessica ignored him. "Or maybe we should go to Venice," she said. "Lila went there, and she's always bragging about how fantastic it was to ride through the canals in a gondola."

"I don't know how much time we'd have for shopping or riding in gondolas," Elizabeth said. "Don't forget, we'd be exchange students. We'd have to go to school." She picked up an application. "I wonder what we have to do to apply."

Jessica snapped her fingers. "How about Acapulco?" she said, her eyes sparkling with excitement.

Elizabeth studied the application for a moment, then put it down with a sigh. "Sorry, Jessica," she said. "We can forget Paris, Venice, and anywhere else you want to go. We don't qualify."

Jessica frowned. "What do you mean? Why not?" she asked.

"It says applicants have to know a second language to be eligible," Elizabeth said. "We're out of luck."

"Is *that* all?" Jessica said airily. "Maybe we could—"

Elizabeth and Steven looked at each other and laughed. "Forget it, Jess," Elizabeth said. "Remember the last time you pretended you knew another language?"

Jessica had tried to win a trip to Paris by entering a contest in *Teenager Magazine*. She'd gotten a little carried away in her description of her family and their knowledge of French culture and language.

Jessica groaned. "Won't you guys ever let me forget that? All I did was tell one tiny fib and my entire family made me feel like an idiot."

"One tiny fib?" Steven said. "What about the part about my being a great jazz trombonist?"

"And Dad being a great painter, and Mom a gourmet cook, and—"

"OK, OK!" Jessica said. "Forget it already!"

"I guess we can forget about GO, too," Elizabeth said. "Too bad. I was really getting to like the idea of three weeks in Paris."

"Hi, gang," Mrs. Wakefield said as she and Mr. Wakefield came through the kitchen door.

"Hi," Elizabeth said.

"How was your jog?" Jessica asked.

"It was terrific," Mrs. Wakefield answered, pouring herself a cup of coffee. "What's this about three weeks in Paris?"

"There's a new foreign exchange program called GO," Jessica explained. "Kids get to spend almost a month in a different country. But since Elizabeth and I don't speak a foreign language, we can't apply."

"Too bad," Mrs. Wakefield said sympathetically. "It sounds like fun. It would be a great way to learn about another culture."

"And do a lot of shopping," Jessica added.

"Well, if you two can't go abroad to learn about a different culture, maybe we can bring it here," Mr. Wakefield suggested.

"What do you mean?" Elizabeth asked.

"We could apply to be a host family," Mr. Wakefield said as he glanced at Mrs. Wakefield. "What do you think?"

"I think it's a great idea," Mrs. Wakefield replied. "We have plenty of room."

"Wait a minute," Steven said, looking alarmed. "You mean, there'd be *another* twelve-year-old girl living here? Twins aren't enough?"

Mr. Wakefield chuckled. "I think you can tough it out, Steven," he said. "Who knows—you might learn something, too."

"So it's agreed?" Elizabeth asked eagerly. "We can apply to be a host family?"

"What are the requirements?" Mr. Wakefield asked.

Elizabeth quickly skimmed the brochure. "All we have to do is fill out a form and have an interview with the coordinator of the program," she answered. "His name is Mr. Lane."

"Sounds easy enough to me," Mr. Wakefield said.

"Let's do it," Mrs. Wakefield added. "Why don't you girls fill out the application today? We can send it to Mr. Lane right away."

"Fantastic!" Jessica exclaimed. "Wait until the Unicorns hear *this*!"

"Triplets," Steven groaned. "What a drag."

"But what exactly does a host family do?" Ellen Riteman asked on Monday morning, after Jessica had told the Unicorns about GO.

Jessica hesitated. She hadn't thought about the details, but it didn't seem very complicated. "We'll just be like the student's own family for a few weeks," she said. "She'll sleep in my room, borrow my clothes, go shopping with me." She smiled. "She'll do everything I do."

"It'll be like having a sister from a different part of the world," Mandy Miller said. "It sounds great, Jessica."

Lila Fowler looked doubtful. "But what if you don't like her?" she asked. "What if she turns out to be a total nerd? What if she doesn't speak English?"

"Yeah," Ellen said. "After all, three weeks is a long time for somebody to live in your room—especially if it's somebody you don't like. And if she comes from somewhere really far away, you can't just tell her to go home again if it doesn't work out."

Jessica tossed her head. "I'll like her," she said confidently. "And she *has* to speak English. It's one of the rules of the program."

Mandy grinned. "What if *she's* a boy?" she asked.

Jessica raised her eyebrows. "A boy? I didn't even think of that!"

"Sure," Mandy replied. "It could just as easily be a boy as a girl, couldn't it?"

"Hmmm . . ." Lila said thoughtfully. "Jessica, maybe you should tell them to send you a guy instead of a girl."

"Maybe he'll be really cute," Ellen said.

Lila snapped her fingers. "I know. We'll have a party for Jessica's exchange student! It's the perfect way to show him all the great things we have here in America: rock music, videos—"

"Pizza and chocolate shakes and hot dogs," Ellen added. "Blue jeans and MTV—"

"And volleyball and skateboarding," Mandy said. "This is going to be really fun. Inviting an exchange student to come to Sweet Valley was *definitely* one of your better ideas, Jessica."

Jessica smiled. "Especially considering that *she* might turn out to be a *he*!"

* * *

On Thursday afternoon, two weeks later, Jessica was in the den watching TV when the phone rang.

"Hello, this is Mr. Lane," a man said. "I'm with the GO program. May I speak to Jessica or Elizabeth Wakefield?"

"I'm Jessica," she said excitedly. "You're the one who interviewed us a couple of weeks ago, right? Have you found an exchange student for us yet?"

"That's what I'm calling about," Mr. Lane replied. "Giovanna Screti, your exchange student, will be arriving next Friday evening from Italy."

"Giovanni Screti!" Jessica exclaimed excitedly. *So it is a boy, after all! How fantastic!* she thought.

"I've mailed some information to you about when and where to pick up your guest and some other details of the visit. You should get it tomorrow."

"Wonderful," Jessica said. "Thanks a lot, Mr. Lane." The minute she put down the phone, she picked it up again to call Lila. Lila was going to be so excited when she heard that the exchange student was a boy! Then suddenly she had a terrible thought. What if Giovanni wasn't a *cute* boy! What if he was a hopeless nerd! She would still have to spend three whole weeks of her life hanging out with him.

"Cute?" Lila said with a laugh, when Jessica mentioned this. "Of course he'll be cute, silly. *All* Italian guys are cute. In fact, when I was in Italy—" She broke off. "You do remember that I was in Italy, don't you?" she asked. "Dad and I spent two whole days in—"

"I know," Jessica said quickly, hoping to forestall an attack of Lila's bragging. She had heard the story of Lila's trip to Italy hundreds of times. "You spent two days in Venice."

"*And* a day in Rome," Lila added. "And everywhere I went in Italy, the guys were absolutely gorgeous." She sighed. "Jessica, I hate to say it, but you are so *lucky* to have an Italian guy staying with you for three whole weeks! I wish *I'd* thought of inviting a foreign student."

When Jessica hung up, she was smiling. She loved making Lila jealous.

"Mr. Lane called," Jessica announced, as soon as the family had sat down at dinner that night. "Our foreign student is named Giovanni Screti. He's from Italy, and he's coming next Friday."

"*He*?" Steven said. "This kid is a guy?" He shrugged. "Well, I guess that's better than another girl."

"Well, this is a surprise," Mrs. Wakefield said. "We'll turn the den into a bedroom for him."

Elizabeth smiled. "Maybe he'll turn out to be a prince in disguise, like Prince Arthur."

Jessica's eyes sparkled. Prince Arthur of Santa Dora had visited Sweet Valley some months before. Everybody thought he was just an ordinary student, but to their surprise he turned out to be the heir to the Santa Doran throne. What if Giovanni was somebody really special—an Italian count, maybe? Lila would be even more jealous!

Mrs. Wakefield smiled. "Prince or no prince," she said, "we'll make sure that Giovanni has a terrific time."

Mr. Wakefield nodded. "If he's going to be sleeping in the den," he said, "we should probably move the TV into the living room."

"Can we give a party?" Jessica asked hopefully. "Maybe a swimming party and cookout one Saturday afternoon."

"Of course," Mrs. Wakefield agreed. She smiled at Jessica and Elizabeth. "I wasn't expecting our exchange student to be a boy. But now that I'm getting used to the idea, I think it will be sort of interesting, don't you?"

Interesting? Jessica said to herself. Having Giovanni there was going to be a lot more than just interesting. She wondered how to say *fabulous* in Italian.

Two

"So how do you feel about having an exchange student that's a boy?" Amy Sutton asked, as she and Elizabeth walked to the Wakefields' house on Friday afternoon.

"Well, Jessica sure is excited about it," Elizabeth answered.

"I know," Amy said, laughing. "I heard the Unicorns talking about it today at lunch. But just because Giovanni is Italian, it doesn't mean he has to be gorgeous, no matter what Lila says."

Elizabeth smiled. "I get the feeling that Lila isn't the expert on Italy that she's pretending to be." She paused. "Can you stay for dinner tonight? I think we're having meat loaf."

"Sure, that would be great," Amy said. "I just have to call my mom."

As she and Amy went inside the house Elizabeth took a handful of mail out of the mailbox. "Look, Amy!" she exclaimed, holding up an envelope. "It's the information Mr. Lane promised to send about Giovanni."

"Open it," Amy urged. "Maybe he sent a picture."

Elizabeth opened the envelope. "No picture," she said. "Just a letter." Elizabeth read it through quickly. The letter explained that Giovanna Screti would be arriving at the Los Angeles International Airport the following Friday night at eight P.M. Elizabeth's eyes widened, and she began to read more slowly. "Giovanna comes from Florence, Italy," she read out loud, "and she is fluent in English. I'm sure you will find her anxious to learn about America and willing to share her life in Italy with you."

"*She*?" Amy asked with a startled look. "*Her* life? I'm confused. I thought she was a he!"

Elizabeth laughed. "Her name is Giovann*a*," she said. "Not Giovann*i*. Jessica must have misunderstood Mr. Lane when he called."

"It's just one letter different. But what a difference!" Amy said. "I wonder what the Unicorns are going to have to say about this!"

Jessica walked into the kitchen just as Mrs. Wakefield was taking the meat loaf out of the oven. "Hi, Mom," she said. "Umm-m, smells good."

"Hello, honey," Mrs. Wakefield replied. "How was school today?"

"Fantastic," Jessica said happily. "Everybody's really excited about Giovanni. Mom, when we give our party, do you think we could invite some seventh and eighth graders too? Everybody wants to meet him."

Mrs. Wakefield smiled. "I don't see why not," she said, "as long as it's not *too* many people. Now, how about setting the table for dinner? Oh, and put out six plates, please. Amy is eating with us tonight."

Jessica frowned. Setting the table was the chore she hated the most. When it was her turn, she always tried to wheedle Elizabeth into doing it for her. "I was just going to call Mandy about something *very* important," she said. "Do you think that maybe Elizabeth—"

"Hi, Jessica," Elizabeth said as she came into

the kitchen with Amy. "You'll never guess what we just—"

"Oh, hi, Elizabeth," Jessica said in her sweetest voice. "Would you mind setting the table for me tonight? I've got this absolutely crucial telephone call to make." She smiled persuasively. "I promise I'll set the table tomorrow night."

"Wait a sec, Jessica," Elizabeth said. "I have to tell you something."

Jessica hurried toward the door. "Thanks, Elizabeth," she yelled over her shoulder.

"Jessica," Elizabeth said. "This crucial call wouldn't be about Giovanni, would it?"

Jessica stopped. "Yeah, why?"

Amy grinned. "Maybe you'd better sit down, Jessica. You're in for a shock."

Jessica looked from Amy to Elizabeth. "What are you talking about?" she demanded. "What kind of a shock?"

Elizabeth held up a sheet of paper. "This is Mr. Lane's letter telling us about our foreign student." She glanced at Jessica. "It turns out that the person we're picking up next Friday is named Giovanna, not Giovanni."

For a moment, no one said anything. Then Mrs. Wakefield raised both eyebrows. "Oh," she said with a little smile. "I see."

"Well, I don't," Jessica said. "So I got the name a little wrong. What does that have to do with anything?"

"Jessica," Elizabeth said, "Giovanna is a *girl's* name."

Jessica stared at Elizabeth. "A *girl*? But Mr. Lane told me—"

"Giovanna is definitely a girl," Elizabeth said.

"It's a mistake anybody could make," Amy added.

Jessica stared at them. "A *girl*," she moaned. She sank down on a chair. "Oh, no! What will Lila say? I'll never live this down!"

"Giovanni, Giovanna—I wish you guys would make up your minds," Steven said that night at dinner.

Mr. Wakefield laughed. "Well," he said, "at least we won't have to make a bedroom out of the den."

"That's right," Elizabeth said. "I'll be glad to have Giovanna sleep in my room. I'm hoping she'll teach me to speak Italian. Maybe I can learn enough to sign up for the GO program myself."

"That's a great idea, Elizabeth," Mrs. Wakefield said.

Jessica frowned. "Wait a minute. What about me?" she asked. "I figured that Giovanna could sleep in my room part of the time, too."

"Now that Giovanna's turned out to be a girl, I didn't think you were interested," Elizabeth replied.

"I'm not *that* disappointed," Jessica said, lifting her chin. "It's not fair for you to hog her all to yourself, Elizabeth."

"But your bedroom is such a mess," Elizabeth argued. "There's not an inch of space to put a cot."

"I can fix that," Jessica said. "I'll clean things up. I'll even do my laundry. That way there'll be *plenty* of room."

"Amazing," Amy muttered.

"*In*-credible," Steven said, rolling his eyes.

Mrs. Wakefield smiled. "I think Jessica is right," she said. "The fair thing is to share our guest between you. Unfortunately, we don't have a cot, but I'm sure we can borrow one. Giovanna can sleep in Elizabeth's bed for a few days, and then in Jessica's, and you girls can sleep on the cot. Then you can trade back again."

"I guess," Jessica said slowly. The Unicorns were going to be disappointed that Giovanna wasn't a guy, but she was trying to look on the bright side. After all, she could do more things with a girl than with a guy. She could take her shopping, for instance, or give her a makeover. *And* they could stay up really late and talk about guys.

"OK, then," Elizabeth said reasonably. "How about if Giovanna sleeps in my room for five days and in your room for five days, and then we trade back." She counted on her fingers. "She's coming on Friday, so that means she'll move in with you the following Wednesday. Is that OK?"

"OK," Jessica agreed. "But it's got to be Wednesday, and not a day later."

"I still don't understand it, Jessica," Lila said as the Unicorns gathered around their regular table at lunch on Monday. "How could you mistake an *a* for an *i*! Only someone who doesn't know any Italian could make a slipup like that. It's simply *ridicolo*." She sat down and opened her milk. "That means 'ridiculous' in Italian, of course."

Jessica rolled her eyes. "Thanks for the lesson, Lila."

"Well," Mandy said, "I think it's going to be fun getting to know an Italian girl. You said she's from Florence, right?"

Lila spoke up before Jessica could answer. "Ah, *Firenze,*" she said, sighing. "The City of Seven Hills. *Bello, bello.* That means 'beautiful,' you know."

"I thought Rome was the City of Seven Hills," Ellen said innocently.

"Well, Florence has a lot of hills, too," Lila replied, narrowing her eyes. "Everybody knows that."

"I wonder what Italian girls are like," Mary Wallace remarked. All the Unicorns looked expectantly at Lila.

"Yeah, Lila," Mandy said. "Tell us about Italian girls."

Lila frowned. "Actually, I didn't pay a lot of attention to the girls there," she said. "But Italian guys are—"

"Tall, dark, handsome," Ellen said with a sigh. "Yes, Lila, we know."

"All this stuff about Italy is getting pretty much out of control," Jessica said.

"Like the Hairnet's unit this week on Mediterranean countries?" Mandy said.

Ellen laughed. "If you're such an expert on Italy, Lila, how come you messed up that question on Amerigo Vespucci today in history?"

Jessica had to laugh at that. Mrs. Arnette had given them a quiz in social studies that morning, and both she and Lila had missed the question about Vespucci, the famous Italian explorer.

"And don't forget we're going to see an Italian opera," Mandy added. "Ms. McDonald is showing her class a videotape of Puccini's famous opera, *Madame Butterfly*."

"Even Mr. Seigel is getting in on the act," Lila said. "He said he was going to talk about Leonardo da Vinci today in science class."

"Speaking of Mr. Seigel," Jessica said, "did you notice that he's over there in the corner, eating lunch with Ms. Wyler?"

"That's interesting," Mandy said, looking in the direction Jessica was pointing. "That's the second time in the past few days I've seen the two of them eating together."

"I wonder what's going on," Ellen said, munching on a carrot stick.

Lila gave a short laugh. "Don't tell me—let me guess. With our luck, he's helping her plan a lecture about famous Italian mathematicians!"

Jessica and Elizabeth hurried home after school on Tuesday to ask their neighbors about borrowing a cot for Giovanna's visit. They started their search with the Howards, who lived next door. But Mrs. Howard shook her head. "You could try Mrs. Cannon, across the street," she suggested.

But Mrs. Cannon wasn't home, and Mr. Mason, next door to her, said they didn't have one. Jessica was beginning to worry that she and Elizabeth might have to sleep on the floor when Mr. Mason came up with a suggestion. "We borrowed a cot from Mrs. Dalone the last time we had company," he said, pointing across the street. "She lives over there on the corner."

Mrs. Dalone's house was small and the yard was filled with bright flowers. "Hello, girls," she said pleasantly, when she answered Elizabeth's knock. She was a plump woman in her sixties, with pretty gray hair. "What can I do for you?"

"My name is Jessica Wakefield," Jessica said,

"and this is my sister, Elizabeth. We live just down the street."

Elizabeth stepped forward. "Mr. Mason said you might have a cot we could borrow," she said. "We're having company for three weeks—a foreign student."

Mrs. Dalone smiled. "I think I have just what you need," she said. She held the door open. "Won't you come in?"

Jessica and Elizabeth followed Mrs. Dalone into a cozy, comfortable living room. There were vases of flowers on the tables, and a calico cat was sunning itself in the window. Mrs. Dalone went to a closet and pulled out a folding cot.

"Is this what you're looking for?" she asked.

"It's perfect," Elizabeth said.

"Where is your foreign student from?" Mrs. Dalone asked.

"From Florence, Italy," Jessica said. "Her name is Giovanna Screti."

"My family is Italian!" Mrs. Dalone exclaimed. "My parents immigrated to America from Sicily, an island off the southern coast of Italy."

"Really?" Jessica asked. "We've been getting really curious about Giovanna—what she'll be like, I mean."

Mrs. Dalone sighed. "I wish I could tell you something about Italian kids," she said, "but I can't. I'm sorry to say I've never been there myself, and I only know the little bit of Italian my mother taught me." She paused, thinking. "But I might have a few pictures, if you'd like to see them."

"That would be great," Jessica said.

Mrs. Dalone took a scrapbook from a bookshelf. "My cousin Anna took these snapshots years ago in the little Sicilian village where my parents were born," she said. "Of course, the people in Sicily are mostly farmers, not city people. So the pictures may not give you what you're looking for." She handed the scrapbook to the twins. "While you're browsing, perhaps you'd like an Italian treat. How about some *spumoni*?"

Jessica frowned doubtfully. "*Spumoni*?" she asked. "I don't think so, thank you."

"*Spumoni* is Italian ice cream," Mrs. Dalone explained. "It's really delicious."

"Ice cream, huh?" Jessica said. "Maybe I will have some. Thank you." Mrs. Dalone smiled and went into the kitchen.

Jessica and Elizabeth sat down on the sofa and opened the scrapbook. "These pictures *are* old," Elizabeth said. "Look how faded and brown they are. The clothes look old-fashioned, too."

Jessica squinted at a brown tinted snapshot of several children with long, stringy hair. They were all barefoot and their clothes were ragged. One girl was leading a goat, and another was carrying a chicken.

Jessica stared at the picture, suddenly apprehensive. "Elizabeth," she whispered, "do you think *all* Italian kids look like this?"

Elizabeth smiled. "Probably not, Jess. These pictures are really old. See, here's one of some kids operating a big wooden machine. What do you think it is?"

Jessica shook her head. She was still looking at the barefoot girl with the goat.

When Mrs. Dalone came back into the living room carrying a tray, Elizabeth asked her about the wooden machine.

"That's a grape crusher," she said. "In the small village my parents came from, children worked right beside the adults. They weeded the fields and took care of the animals and did lots of other chores. In that photo, they're helping to make wine. Some of the best grapes in the world grow in Italy, you know."

Jessica gave Mrs. Dalone a doubtful look. "Children *work*?" she asked. "But what about school?"

Mrs. Dalone shook her head. "That's why my parents came to America. They loved Italy, but back then there wasn't much chance for their children to get an education, and they wanted to build a better life for their family. When they left the village, there wasn't even any indoor plumbing. I can remember my mother saying that America was the land of opportunity and electric lights."

"I see," Jessica said, closing the scrapbook. Italian children in rags, barefoot? Was that how Giovanna would look? Of course, the photos *had* been taken a while ago, and times had changed since then. But had times changed all that much? Maybe Giovanna wanted to visit America because it was still the land of opportunity, just the way it had been when Mrs. Dalone's parents immigrated.

Mrs. Dalone handed Jessica a bowl and a spoon. "Here, Jessica. Try some *spumoni*."

The *spumoni* was white, like vanilla ice cream,

and speckled with little colored flecks. Jessica took a tiny taste. It was delicious. "Mmm-mm," she said.

When the twins were finished with their ice cream, they thanked Mrs. Dalone for loaning them the cot.

"When Giovanna comes, please bring her to visit me," Mrs. Dalone told them as they said good-bye. "Just thinking about Italy is exciting for me. I could even practice some of my rusty Italian on her."

"We'll bring her over as soon as we can," Elizabeth promised.

"*Bene,*" Mrs. Dalone said. "That's Italian for 'good.' "

"*Ciao,*" Jessica said with a wave.

"Elizabeth," Jessica said a little later, as they were setting up the cot in Elizabeth's room, "I was wondering, do you think . . ." Her voice trailed off. "Do you think Giovanna has a goat?" she finally blurted out.

Elizabeth laughed. "Jessica, those pictures showed the way people lived a long time ago. Things are different now. And anyway, Giovanna lives in a big city. It would probably be even harder for her to have a goat in Florence than it would be for us to have one in Sweet Valley."

"I guess," Jessica said. "But I'm beginning to wonder just how different Giovanna is going to be. After all, she comes from a foreign country, and she speaks a foreign language. Her clothes will be different, her hair, the way she thinks, the way she talks."

"But that's the whole reason for inviting a foreign student to stay with us," Elizabeth reminded her. "Giovanna *will* be different. We can learn a lot from her, and she'll learn a lot from us, too."

"You might be right," Jessica said thoughtfully. "I could teach her a lot about clothes and makeup. In fact, I could give her a total makeover."

Elizabeth looked doubtful. "I guess so, if that's what Giovanna wants."

"But of *course* Giovanna will want a makeover," Jessica replied quickly. "If she's anything like those kids in the picture she'll *need* one."

Three

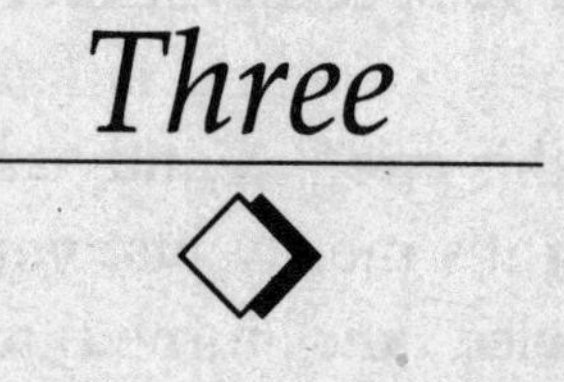

"What are those, Lila?" Jessica asked as she, Ellen, Mandy, and Lila sat down around a library table on Friday.

"These are pictures from my trip to Rome," Lila said, putting a stack of photos on the table. "I thought maybe we could use them in our report on Italy." Mrs. Arnette had assigned group reports to the social studies class, and sent them to the library to do research. Lila picked up a photo. "Oh, I love this one. This is me standing in front of the Coliseum—"

"It's only half a coliseum," Ellen said, looking at the picture. "Part of it is gone."

"Of course it's gone, dummy," Lila snapped. "Most of it fell down a long time ago. It's *ancient*."

She put her finger on another picture. "This is me on a bridge across the Tiber River. Isn't that a cute outfit? It's a genuine Ricci. It cost a fortune in *lire*. That's Italian money," she added. "Dad gave me a bunch of *lire* to spend on clothes when we were in Rome."

"What's this one?" Mandy asked. "I think it's your dad, but it's mostly just your thumb."

Lila scowled and turned to the next one. "Here I am buying flowers from a vendor in the market," she said. She looked dreamily at the photo. "Isn't he cute? He kind of reminds me of Jake Hamilton."

Mandy laughed. "Lila, *all* cute boys remind you of Jake."

Ellen threw down her pencil. "You know, I'm getting pretty sick of all this Italian stuff—writing this report and listening to opera and hearing about your trip. What's so special about Italy, anyway? I'm so tired of talking about it!"

"Don't worry about what Ellen said," Mandy said a few minutes later as she and Jessica walked out of the library. "She's just jealous of Lila's trip to Italy." She grinned. "I'm a little tired of hearing about it, myself. Lila never knows when to shut up."

"I know," Jessica said. "But I'm really beginning to worry. Maybe nobody will like Giovanna. Maybe she'll look so different that—"

Mandy grinned. "Quit worrying so much, Jessica. Anyway, it doesn't matter what she looks like. What matters is—" She broke off as they turned the corner by their lockers. "Hey, look," she said. "It's Mr. Seigel with Ms. Wyler again."

Jessica noticed the two teachers were standing close together, whispering. At that moment, Ms. Wyler glanced up and saw Jessica and Mandy, and she and Mr. Seigel stepped into Ms. Wyler's room and shut the door behind them.

"If you ask me," Mandy said, "they've got some sort of deep, dark secret." She giggled. "And I don't think it's got anything to do with Italian mathematicians, either. What do you think they're up to?"

Jessica stared after them. "I wish I knew."

"All aboard for the airport," Mr. Wakefield called from the driveway that Friday night.

"I don't see why I have to go," Steven grumbled as he climbed into the Wakefields' van. "Having an exchange student wasn't *my* idea."

"We're all going because this is a family

project," Mrs. Wakefield said, getting into the front seat. "You're going to learn as much from Giovanna as the rest of us."

"Anyway," Mr. Wakefield said, starting the van, "Giovanna will probably feel a lot more welcome if we're all there to meet her. After all, coming to America must be a big occasion for her. I wouldn't be surprised if she's a little anxious about meeting us."

"Anxious about meeting us?" Jessica asked. "*We're* the ones who are anxious. I wonder what she's like."

"You sound like a broken record, Jess," Steven said. "You've said that three times in the last hour."

"Well, I can't help it," Jessica replied defensively. "Giovanna's going to live with us for three whole weeks. That's a long time."

"And she's going to be in *my* room half the time," Elizabeth said excitedly. "I hope she's not too tired when she gets here—I have a million questions. I'm ready to talk all night."

At the airport, Mr. Wakefield parked the van in the lot and they all went inside to wait. After fifteen minutes, a woman announced over a microphone that Giovanna's plane had arrived. The

Wakefields gathered at the end of a hallway to greet her.

"How are we supposed to recognize her?" Steven asked, as passengers began to stream down the hallway.

"Mr. Lane said in his letter that she'd be wearing a GO button," Mrs. Wakefield said, as they watched several girls come down the ramp together, carrying small suitcases and chattering in what Jessica assumed was Italian.

Jessica's heart leaped. The girls looked completely normal. She pointed. "Maybe she's one of them," she said hopefully.

Elizabeth shook her head. "None of them is wearing a GO button."

A second large group of passengers came down the ramp, and then a third, and still no Giovanna.

"Maybe she missed the flight," Steven speculated. "Or maybe she decided she didn't want to come after all. Maybe she caught sight of you two and ran in the other direction!"

"Very funny, Steven," Jessica said dryly.

"I'm sure she'll be along any minute," Mrs. Wakefield assured them. "It must be a big plane."

Mr. Wakefield peered into the crowd. "I think

I see her," he said. "Yes, there she is!" He pointed toward the last group of people moving down the ramp.

Jessica stood on tiptoe. When she finally spotted the girl with a big red-and-white GO button on her shoulder, she could hardly believe her eyes. Elizabeth sucked in her breath, and Steven let out a whistle.

"Wow!" he said, half under his breath. "*That's* Giovanna?"

"Giovanna!" Elizabeth called, waving. "Here we are!"

Jessica opened her mouth to call out, too, but all that came out was a croak. For once in her life, Jessica was speechless.

Giovanna smiled and walked toward them. She was as tall and elegant as a fashion model. She had beautiful olive skin, clear hazel eyes, and long dark hair that swung around her shoulders. To top it off, she was wearing a black leather jacket that Jessica had fallen in love with when she'd seen it in *Image* magazine.

Jessica swallowed. She could forget about the makeover, and about teaching Giovanna what clothes to wear. Giovanna could probably teach *her* a thing or two!

"Welcome to Sweet Valley, Giovanna," Mrs. Wakefield said warmly. "We're so glad that you're here!"

Giovanna gave her a polite smile. "Do you remain well, *signora*?" she asked, with a strong accent.

"Yes, thank you," Mrs. Wakefield said as she shook Giovanna's hand. "This is Mr. Wakefield," she said. She turned to the twins. "And here are Jessica, Elizabeth, and Steven. They've been very excited about your arrival."

Giovanna looked at Jessica, and then at Elizabeth, frowning a little. Jessica laughed. "We're identical twins," she said. "It's easy to mix us up at first, but when you get to know us you'll see we're really different."

Giovanna laughed. "I expect to have a wonderful time in America," she said brightly.

Steven stepped forward eagerly. "That suitcase looks heavy," he said, reaching for her bag. "Let me give you a hand."

Giovanna looked confused. "Do you not need your hand?" she asked. She reached down and picked up her suitcase. "It makes bad weather today," she continued, speaking to Jessica. "Is it not so, Elizabeth?"

Jessica shifted uncomfortably. It sounded as if Giovanna was reciting phrases out of a guidebook, but she wasn't quite getting them right. "Well, actually," she said, "the weather has been pretty nice lately. And I'm Jessica."

"Thank you very much," Giovanna replied. She smiled at Jessica. "It is a pleasure to meet you. I hope you are well."

Mr. Wakefield cleared his throat. "Giovanna, did you bring other luggage?" he asked very slowly and clearly. He pointed to her suitcase. "Other bags?"

Giovanna gave him a perplexed look, then her face cleared. "Ah, *si*," she said triumphantly, "*bagaglio*. Bags. *Si*." She pulled out her plane ticket with two baggage stubs attached and handed it to Mr. Wakefield.

"If you ask me," Jessica whispered, as she and Elizabeth followed Giovanna and the rest of the family to the baggage carousel, "Giovanna must have exaggerated when she told the people at GO she could speak English."

Elizabeth nodded, looking worried. "You might be right," she said. "But maybe Giovanna's just tired. After all, she's had a long day."

"But what if she really *can't* speak English?"

Jessica asked apprehensively. "What if we have to spend every minute of the next three weeks just trying to understand her?"

"Well, it's got to be harder on her than it is on us," Elizabeth said reasonably. "After all, English is our language, and Sweet Valley is our hometown. She's trying to cope with a language she doesn't understand very well, in a place she's never been before. If I were in her shoes right now, I'll bet I'd be scared."

Jessica shook her head skeptically. Giovanna was standing off to the side, one hand on her hip.

"She doesn't look very scared to me," Jessica said, glancing enviously at Giovanna's outfit. "She may not understand much English, Elizabeth, but there's one language she's fluent in."

"What's that?"

Jessica sighed. "The language of fashion."

Four

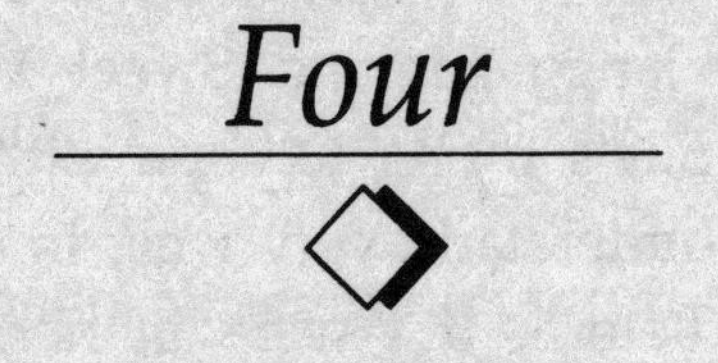

"Is there enough hot chocolate for me, Jess?" Elizabeth asked. It was nearly ten that night and she had come down to the kitchen to fix herself a snack. Jessica was there, making hot chocolate.

"I've fixed enough for three," Jessica said. "I thought Giovanna might like some. I wonder if they drink hot chocolate in Italy."

"Giovanna's already gone to bed," Elizabeth said, opening the refrigerator.

Jessica poured the chocolate into two cups and added a dollop of whipped cream to each. "You sound disappointed," she said.

"I guess I am," Elizabeth replied. She put some chocolate chip cookies on a plate and sat down at the table. "I was looking forward to a nice long talk while Giovanna unpacked and got settled. But she was so tired that she just crawled into bed and pulled the covers over her head without saying more than two or three words."

"In which language?" Jessica asked, sitting down at the table.

Elizabeth sat down, too. "I still think she's just tired, Jess. I'm sure she'll be thinking a lot more clearly in the morning, and her English will probably be better."

Jessica looked thoughtful. "I can't wait to see the rest of the clothes she's got packed in those suitcases," she said. "When Lila sees that black leather jacket, she will absolutely die."

Elizabeth laughed. "So no makeover for Giovanna, huh?"

Jessica shook her head. "Maybe she'll give me one."

"Do you still think she has a pet goat?" Elizabeth joked.

Jessica laughed. "I *highly* doubt it!"

When she woke up the next morning, Elizabeth lay still for a minute, trying to recall why she was sleeping in a different corner of the room. Then she remembered and sat straight up on the cot. In the bed on the other side of the room, Giovanna stretched and yawned.

"Good morning, Giovanna," Elizabeth said. She rubbed her back. Mrs. Dalone's cot wasn't as soft as it looked.

"*Buon giorno*, Elizabeth," Giovanna said, tossing her long dark hair back over her shoulders. Then she smiled. "Good morning, I mean. Pardon, please. I forget that it is good to speak English while I am in America."

Elizabeth gave a sigh of relief. So Giovanna *could* speak some English, at least. "I'll bet you're hungry for breakfast," she said slowly, pronouncing every word. "And after breakfast, some friends are coming over to meet you—Maria Slater and Mandy Miller." She and Jessica had thought about asking a few other people, but had decided that it might be a good thing not to start off with a crowd.

"Ah, breakfast," Giovanna said, rubbing her stomach. "*Bene.*" She tossed the covers back and jumped out of bed. She opened her suitcase and pulled out two or three things, tossing them on the floor.

"Do you want to hang your clothes in the closet?" Elizabeth asked, climbing into a pair of khaki shorts. She went to the closet door and opened it, pointing to the space she had cleared for Giovanna. "Closet," she repeated. "For your clothes."

Giovanna shook her head firmly. "It is better to eat breakfast first," she said, still rummaging in her suitcase. Finally she found what she was looking for, a short white pleated skirt and a black T-shirt that said *Italia!* on the front in jagged red letters.

Elizabeth had put on a pink T-shirt and brushed her long blond hair into a ponytail by the time Giovanna came out of the bathroom, frowning.

"I did not bring my—how you say, my . . ." She made a combing motion with her hand.

"Comb?" Elizabeth said. She found hers and held it up. Then she picked up her hairbrush. "Hairbrush?"

Giovanna broke into a wide smile. "Ah, yes, hairbrush," she said. "*Grazie*."

Grazie, Elizabeth figured, must mean "thank you." "You're welcome," she said with a smile, as Giovanna disappeared into the bathroom with Elizabeth's hairbrush and a makeup kit from her suitcase.

When the girls got down to the kitchen, Mrs. Wakefield was already there, frying bacon. "Good morning, Giovanna," she said. "Hi, Elizabeth."

"Good morning," Giovanna said.

Elizabeth grinned. "*Buon giorno,*" she told her mother.

Mrs. Wakefield smiled. "*Buon giorno,*" she said.

Jessica came into the kitchen from the den, dressed in denim shorts and a purple top. Her hair was pulled back with a blue hair band. "Hi, Mom. Hi, Elizabeth," she said cheerfully. "Good morning, Giovanna." She examined Giovanna's outfit. "Wow, you look great."

"Giovanna," Mrs. Wakefield said, "would you like one or two eggs for breakfast?"

Giovanna frowned at Mrs. Wakefield. "Eggs?" she asked.

Elizabeth picked up an egg. "Egg," she said. "One or two?" she asked.

Giovanna shook her head. "No eggs," she said firmly. "In Italy, we do not eat eggs for breakfast."

"You don't eat eggs?" Jessica asked in surprise. "What *do* you eat? Pancakes?"

Giovanna looked confused. "Pan-cakes?" she asked slowly. "This is a cake made in a pan?"

Elizabeth went to the pantry and found the box of pancake mix, with a picture on it. When she held it up, Giovanna's expression cleared.

"Oh," she said, "*fritelle*. Yes, sometimes I eat the pancakes." She sat down at the table and folded her hands in her lap. "But in Italy, always we eat fresh fruit for breakfast."

"That's interesting," Mrs. Wakefield said. She turned to Jessica. "I think we might have some strawberries in the refrigerator. Would you take a look?"

"Straw-berries?" Giovanna asked. She wrinkled her nose distastefully. "These are berries in the straw?"

Jessica laughed as she went to the refrigerator and pulled out a plastic box. "Here they are. Would you like some? I could fix them with sugar and cream," she said cheerfully.

"Ah, *fragole*," Giovanna said with a smile of recognition. Carefully, she pinched one berry, then sniffed the others and sat back. "Thank you," she said, shaking her head. "But fruit must be fresh."

Elizabeth and Jessica exchanged looks. Then Elizabeth went to the cupboard to see what kind of cereal she could find. "How about a bowl of Cream of Wheat?" she asked. "Or corn flakes."

"Cream and wheat?" Giovanna asked, puzzled. "Flakes of corn? What are these things? I do not understand." Finally, after some explanation, Giovanna settled for pancakes.

Feeling somewhat exasperated, Elizabeth mixed up a batch while Jessica gave Giovanna a language lesson.

"We'll start with easy things first," Jessica said. "Plate, knife, fork, spoon."

"Plate," Giovanna repeated. "Knife, fork, spoon."

"Toaster, coffee maker," Jessica said, working her way around the counter. "Microwave oven." Then she paused. "Maybe they don't have microwaves in Italy."

Giovanna gave a laugh. "Of course we have these," she said. "In our house, for our *cuoca*."

"Your *cuoca*?" Elizabeth asked.

"*Si*," Giovanna said, making a motion as if she were stirring something in a bowl.

Mrs. Wakefield smiled. "I think Giovanna is telling us that her family has a cook."

"Oh," Jessica replied. She laughed uneasily. "Maybe Giovanna and Lila have more in common than I thought."

Just then, Steven came into the kitchen, rubbing his eyes sleepily. "Good morning," he mumbled. "Hi, Giovanna," he said, looking a little more alert.

"Steven, your eggs are ready," Mrs. Wakefield said.

"Good morning, Giovanna," Mr. Wakefield said, coming in. "I hope you slept well last night."

"Good morning, *signore*," Giovanna said carefully. "I sleep well, thank you."

Mrs. Wakefield smiled. "Would you like some coffee, Ned?"

Giovanna brightened. "I will have coffee, too," she said.

Mr. and Mrs. Wakefield looked at each other. "Do you drink coffee at home, Giovanna?" Mrs. Wakefield asked.

"Of course," Giovanna said, arching her eyebrows. "In Italy, all people drink coffee, except for *bambini*."

"*Bambini*?" Elizabeth asked.

"*Bambini* are little children," Mrs. Wakefield explained.

Giovanna glanced at Elizabeth's glass of milk. "You do not drink coffee, Elizabeth?"

Elizabeth shook her head, feeling very immature. She could tell by the look on Jessica's face that she felt the same way.

Giovanna tasted her coffee. "This coffee is different," she said, wrinkling her nose.

Giovanna put her cup down, noticing the basketball under Steven's arm. "You play the basketball, Steven?" she asked.

"Yeah, I'm on the Sweet Valley High junior varsity," he said proudly.

Giovanna leaned forward. "Are you a big star?" she asked eagerly.

Steven gave her a modest smile. "I don't know about being a big star," he said, sitting down to eat his egg. "But I'm OK. Hey, how about a hoop lesson after breakfast?"

"A hoop lesson?" Giovanna asked. She frowned. "This is a lesson in how to make the hoops?"

"He means a basketball lesson," Elizabeth explained.

Giovanna clapped her hands delightedly. "Of course!" she cried. "In Italy, we love the basketball very much."

So after breakfast, while Jessica and Elizabeth helped Mr. and Mrs. Wakefield clean up the kitchen, Giovanna went outside with Steven. In a minute, they could hear the basketball bouncing against the backboard, and the sound of laughter.

"I guess Giovanna didn't like my pancakes," Elizabeth said, scraping several off her plate and into the garbage.

"Maybe they just didn't taste the way they do in Italy," Jessica replied.

"Hi, Maria," Jessica said an hour or so later, when she answered the doorbell. "Hi, Mandy. Come on in and meet Giovanna."

"Hi, Giovanna," Maria said, when Jessica and Elizabeth introduced them. "Welcome to America!" With a little bow, she handed Giovanna a tiny American flag.

"We're really glad you're here," Mandy said. "It's going to be a lot of fun, showing you all the sights."

"This is good, thank you," Giovanna said. "Seeing sights is an enjoyable occupation, is it not?"

Mandy looked a little confused.

"Listen, you guys," Jessica said, "we're having a pool party next Saturday."

"A pool party?" Maria asked. "That's great! I'll bring over my new tapes."

Giovanna smiled. "I think that is very great, Jessica. My friends have taught me to play the pool."

"Play the pool?" Jessica asked, frowning.

"But where is the pool table?" Giovanna asked. "I have not seen it anywhere."

Elizabeth laughed. "We're talking about a party around our swimming pool," she said, pointing toward the backyard.

"Hey, let's get going," Jessica said. "Why don't we take a walk downtown so Giovanna can get a look at Sweet Valley."

"Good idea," Elizabeth said. "I'll get my camera and we can take pictures. Giovanna might want to take them back to Italy with her."

Giovanna smiled. "That is a very fine idea, Elizabeth," she said. "My friends in Italy are very interested in America."

The walk was fun, and Giovanna's English seemed to be improving quickly.

"You have such *big* cars in America," Giovanna remarked at one point. "And trucks." She pointed to a line of cars and trucks waiting for a stoplight. "In Florence, our streets are narrow. Big cars take up too much room. They make . . ." She gestured. "How do you say it? Jelly of the traffic?"

Jessica couldn't help giggling. "Traffic jelly. That's the best description I've ever heard. Giovanna, just wait until you see the traffic jelly in L.A.!" They all laughed.

Giovanna looked puzzled. "Do I make the joke?" she asked, sounding a little hurt.

"Not really," Elizabeth said with a smile. "But you probably mean traffic *jam,* not jelly."

Giovanna nodded. "Yes," she said with satisfaction. "Traffic jams. Thank you, Elizabeth."

"If people don't have cars, how do they get around?" Maria asked.

"They walk," Giovanna replied. "Many ride the bus. Of course," she added, "I ride my scooter."

"You have a scooter?" Jessica asked enviously.

"Awesome," Mandy whispered.

Jessica frowned. Giovanna drank coffee, wore cool, expensive clothes, and rode a scooter. Compared to her, Jessica was beginning to feel like a little kid. And it wasn't a feeling she liked at all.

Giovanna turned to Mandy. "Awe-some?" she asked. "What is this?"

"It means amazing," Maria explained.

"It is awe-some to have a scooter?" Giovanna asked. "You do not have scooters? How do you get to school?"

Mandy heaved a sigh. "We walk," she said.

Giovanna shook her head with a pitying look. "In Italy, all my friends have scooters. We ride them everywhere."

Jessica decided it was time to change the subject. "That's our new civic center over there," she said, pointing. "It was just built last year. And that's our new library next to the post office. It's not quite finished."

Giovanna looked around. "But where are your ancient buildings?" she asked. She lifted her chin. "In Italy, we are proud of what is old."

"We're proud of our old buildings, too," Jessica said defensively. She pointed across the park. "See that Spanish mission over there behind the palm trees? It's so old, it might fall down!"

"That's right," Maria added. "It's the oldest building in town. It's over two hundred years old."

"Two hundred years?" Giovanna asked with amusement. "The Pantheon is over *two thousand* years old."

There was a long silence.

"It's about time you built a new one," Jessica said finally.

The one thing in Sweet Valley that did impress Giovanna was the size of the office buildings. "This is truly awe-some," she said, as she stared up at a building that was only about fifteen stories high.

"But that isn't a big building," Jessica protested. "There are hundreds of skyscrapers in Los Angeles that are a lot taller."

Giovanna blinked. "They scrape the sky?"

"Well, not really," Elizabeth replied with a laugh. "That's just what they're called."

Giovanna looked up at the office building again. "This one must scrape the sky," she said. "In Italy, we do not have such tall buildings. But I am glad. Very tall buildings would make our ancient buildings look very small."

Jessica shook her head. *Italy's weird,* she thought to herself. *And Giovanna is even weirder.*

"Hi, Jess."

Jessica turned around to see Aaron Dallas coming toward them from the direction of the Dairi Burger.

"Hi, Aaron," she said with a smile, but Aaron's attention was already focused on Giovanna.

"You must be Giovanna—the girl we thought was a guy," he said.

Giovanna smiled as Jessica introduced them. "I am most happy to meet you, Aaron," she said. "But how was it that you thought I was a boy?"

"That was Jessica's mistake," Aaron said. He smiled at Giovanna. "Nobody would ever mistake *you* for a guy."

Inside, Jessica was beginning to fume.

"Thank you," Giovanna said demurely. "You are very nice."

As soon as Aaron had left, Giovanna turned to Jessica. "Are all American boys as good-looking as your friend Aaron?"

"Yeah," Jessica said. "In fact, you don't want to waste your time on him. I'll be glad to introduce you to some of the *really* cute ones."

Mandy laughed.

"Awe-some," Giovanna said.

Five

"Jessica," Elizabeth called anxiously from the dining room, "is everything ready?"

"Yes," Jessica said, coming in from the kitchen with a heavy bowl. "It looks great, Elizabeth," she said as she surveyed the table. "An authentic Italian feast."

"I hope Giovanna will think so," Elizabeth said. "I especially like the Italian flag you made for a centerpiece." She checked the table once more to be sure that she and Jessica hadn't forgotten anything. They had spent all afternoon making spaghetti and meatballs with a special Italian tomato sauce, garlic bread, and a salad with Italian dressing.

"Your dinner looks delicious, girls," Mrs.

Wakefield said, coming into the dining room. "I'm sure Giovanna will be impressed."

Elizabeth sighed. "I don't know. The only thing that's impressed her so far were a few tall buildings."

"And Aaron," Jessica muttered, folding the napkins.

A few minutes later, all the Wakefields and Giovanna were seated around the table. "That's a great-looking Italian flag, Jessica," Mr. Wakefield said, admiring the centerpiece.

Giovanna cleared her throat. "Excuse me," she said. "That is not the flag of Italy."

"But I copied it from the encyclopedia," Jessica protested. "Red, white, and green."

"The flag of Italy is green, white, and red," Giovanna explained. "The green is first. This flag is—how do you say it?—back-sided?"

"Backwards," Steven corrected. "Better luck next time, shrimp." He grinned teasingly at Jessica. "But I have to say that you and Elizabeth do know how to cook spaghetti."

Elizabeth turned to Giovanna. "What do you think? Does it taste like real Italian spaghetti?"

Giovanna tasted her spaghetti. Then she hesitated for a moment. "No," she said finally. "It is different."

"Different?" Elizabeth asked. "But we got the recipe from an Italian cookbook."

Giovanna tasted her sauce once again. "Were the tomatoes fresh?" she asked.

Elizabeth shook her head. "I used canned ones. The recipe said those were good, too."

"In Italy," Giovanna said, "the sauce tastes like fresh tomatoes." She poked at her meatballs. "The meatballs and sauce are served in separate dishes. And the spaghetti is . . ." She held up her fork, a strand of spaghetti dangling from it limply. "More chewy."

"Who wants chewy spaghetti?" Jessica asked defensively. She took a big bite of salad. "The salad is terrific, Elizabeth. Very Italian."

Mr. Wakefield looked up. "The garlic bread is very good, too," he said, reaching for a second piece.

"In Italy," Giovanna remarked, "we eat the salad last, and we *always* drink wine." She eyed the green shaker-can of Parmesan cheese in front of her. "*Parmigiano* does not come in green cans. And the bread is . . ." She looked pointedly at the long loaf of bread in front of Mr. Wakefield. "The bread is not *French*."

"You drink wine?" Steven asked.

"Of course I drink wine," Giovanna said. "In Italy, *everyone* drinks wine, even the *bambini*."

Elizabeth and Jessica exchanged glances.

"Dad," Jessica began.

"Don't even think about it," Mr. Wakefield said with a laugh.

"Where's Giovanna?" Amy asked Elizabeth on Monday morning. They were standing in front of Elizabeth's locker at school.

"She's with Jessica," Elizabeth said, taking her English book out of her locker. "You can meet her in homeroom."

"I'm sorry I couldn't get together with you this weekend," Amy said. "My grandma was here. How did things go?"

Elizabeth shrugged. "Pretty much OK," she said, "except that we've got a language problem. Giovanna's English isn't very good."

"No kidding?" Amy asked.

"We had a few other problems, too. At dinner Saturday night, Jessica mixed up the colors on the Italian flag. And our authentic Italian meal wasn't really Italian because the spaghetti wasn't chewy and the tomatoes weren't fresh and the bread happened to be French."

Amy giggled. "Well, at least you tried."

Elizabeth nodded. "To be fair, she might not have said anything if I hadn't asked her opinion." She closed her locker.

"What's it like to have her as a roommate?" Amy asked as they walked in the direction of homeroom.

"It's a lot like sharing a room with Jessica," Elizabeth said ruefully. "I made room for her clothes in the closet, but she leaves them lying around everywhere. She only moved in Friday night, but already it's hard to find a place to walk."

"She and Jessica are going to make a great team," Amy said. "When does she move to Jessica's room?"

"On Wednesday," Elizabeth said. "I hate to admit it, but I'm already looking forward to it."

"Lila, Ellen," Jessica said, "I'd like you to meet Giovanna." She grinned, waiting to see how they'd react. Giovanna was wearing black leather pants and boots, a silky gold top, huge hoop earrings, and more makeup than most middle schoolers wore. Next to her, the usually fashionable Lila and Ellen looked almost nerdy.

Ellen's eyes widened. "H-hi, Giovanna," she stammered, staring enviously at Giovanna's leather pants.

"It is kind to make your acquaintance," Giovanna said in her heavily accented voice. Jessica noticed that she made more mistakes when she first met people, maybe because she was nervous.

Lila stepped forward. "*Buon giorno,* Giovanna," she said loudly. "*Mi chiamo* Lila Fowler."

"What'd she say?" Jessica whispered to Ellen.

"She said, 'Good morning, my name is Lila Fowler,' " Ellen whispered back. "She looked it up in an Italian book. She's been practicing it all weekend."

Giovanna smiled at Lila and spoke a stream of rapid Italian, then paused and waited for Lila to answer.

Lila blinked. "You'll have to go slower," she said, looking embarrassed. "I'm afraid my Italian is a little rusty."

Giovanna said something else in Italian, very slowly, and Lila shook her head, biting her lip.

Giovanna paused. "You do not speak Italian at all?"

"Bingo," Ellen whispered to Jessica.

Lila's face turned pink. "Maybe I don't know much Italian," she said. "But I *have* traveled to Italy. I've been in lots of Italian cities."

"Did you enjoy Florence?" Giovanna asked politely. "That is where I live. It is a very beautiful city."

"We, uh, actually, we didn't go to Florence," Lila said.

"You must have gone to Pisa, then," Giovanna said, "to see the Leaning Tower." She laughed a little. "All the American tourists want to take a picture of the Leaning Tower. And they always go to Tuscany, to visit the beautiful wine country. Did you enjoy Tuscany?"

By this time, Lila's face was deep red. "We didn't go to Pisa," she said. "Or Tuscany. But we *did* go to Venice and Rome." She gestured at her outfit. "I bought this in Rome."

Giovanna waved her hand. "Of course," she said. "All the tourists feel they must ride in a gondola and spend a few *lire* on Italian clothes." She smiled politely. "Someday I hope you will come back and see what Italy is really like."

Jessica could see that Lila was seething. She was so angry, in fact, that she didn't notice Jake Hamilton until he was standing right beside her.

"Hi, Lila," Jake said casually. He grinned at Giovanna. "Hey, why don't you introduce me to your friend?"

Lila tried to smile at Jake. "She's Jessica's friend," she said between clenched teeth.

"Giovanna," Jessica said, "this is Jake Hamilton. He's a big basketball star. Jake, this is Giovanna Screti. She's from Italy."

Jake grinned at Giovanna. "I've always heard people say that Italian girls are very cool," he said.

Giovanna frowned a little. "Very cool?" she asked.

Lila cleared her throat. "Uh, listen, you guys, it's almost time for the bell. Don't you think we'd better get going before Mr. Davis—"

Giovanna smiled at Jake. "So it is good in America to be 'very cool'?"

"Sure, it's good," Jake said. "So how do you like it here in America?"

"America is beautiful," Giovanna said, "and the boys are very handsome."

Jake looked pleased.

Lila opened her mouth, but nothing came out.

"You are truly a big basketball star, Jake?" she asked.

Jake tried to look modest. "I've been known to score a few points," he said.

"That is very cool," Giovanna murmured. "Maybe you would be so kind as to give me the hop lesson."

Jake looked puzzled. "Hop lesson?"

Lila gave a loud snicker. "Maybe you'd better have an English lesson instead."

"My English is not so perfect," Giovanna said frostily. "But I think it is better than your Italian."

"I think Giovanna means 'hoop' lesson," Jessica said to Jake. "My brother, Steven, gave her a few basketball pointers on Saturday morning."

"Oh, sure, a hoop lesson. Fantastic! How about meeting me at the cafeteria at noon, Giovanna? We'll grab a sandwich and then head for the courts," Jake said happily.

Giovanna looked at Jessica. "It is permitted to grab the sandwich?" she asked, frowning. "It is not stealing?"

"He just means that he wants to eat fast," Jessica said.

Giovanna turned to Jake. "It is kind of you to invite me to grab the sandwich," she said. "I would enjoy that very much."

"Then it's a date," Jake said.

Lila stepped closer to Jake. "Ellen and Jessica and I would enjoy it, too, Jake," she said sweetly. "We always *adore* watching you play basketball."

Jake looked flattered. "No kidding?" he asked. "Sure, you can come along if you want to," he said as he headed down the hall.

Giovanna turned to Jessica. "No kid-ding?" she asked. "What does Jake mean when he says 'no kid-ding'?"

"It's what you say when you want to be sure about something," Jessica said. "If somebody's not kidding, it means they're telling the truth."

Giovanna put her hands on her hips. "Jake Hamilton is a very handsome boy, no kid-ding?"

"No kidding," Jessica said, with a glance at Lila.

"What did you do that for?" Lila hissed when Ellen and Giovanna went into the classroom.

"Do what for?" Jessica asked innocently.

"Why did you introduce Jake as a big star?"

Lila asked, stamping her foot. "You practically threw him at Giovanna. And she was only too eager to take advantage of him."

"Take advantage of him?" Jessica asked. "Jake asked *her* to lunch."

"Maybe so," Lila said darkly, "but he wouldn't have if she hadn't begged him to give her a *hop* lesson." She gave a short, sarcastic laugh. "Can you believe she would wear an outfit like that to school? And all that makeup?"

"I think she looks great," Jessica replied. "Anyway, Italian girls act older than American girls. In Italy, Giovanna drinks coffee and wine and rides her own scooter."

"Her very own scooter?" Lila asked. She shook her head. "Jessica, *nobody* our age has a scooter. It's against the law. Giovanna Screti is telling you a big fat bunch of lies, and you've completely fallen for them."

"It's against the law *here*," Jessica replied, "but that doesn't mean it's against the law in Italy." She tossed her head. "And if you ask me, Jake is the one who's falling."

Six

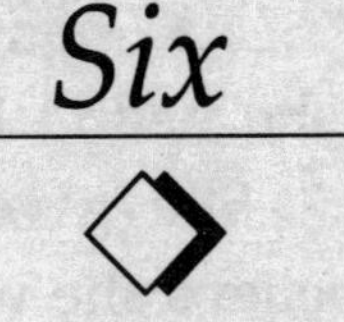

"That was wonderful, Giovanna," Mr. Bowman said, as Giovanna finished reading an Italian poem to the English class.

Jessica had to admit that Giovanna's Italian had sounded very impressive, even though she couldn't understand a word.

Mr. Bowman smiled. "Now that you've given us such a terrific introduction to the Italian language, Giovanna, how about telling us a little about your reactions to America?"

Giovanna lowered her eyes. "My English is not so good," she muttered. "Especially when I have to talk to many people. I am—how do you say it? Stagestruck?"

Lila snickered.

Mr. Bowman smiled. "I think you mean that you have stage fright," he said. "In that case, how about writing something down and reading it to us? You could do it next week. That'll give you a little more time to see the sights and decide what you think about this country of ours. How does that sound?"

"That sounds good," Giovanna said, nodding. "I will do it, no kid-ding."

Mr. Bowman grinned. "*Grazie*," he said. He turned to the class. "That means 'thanks' in Italian."

Giovanna smiled back. "*Prego*," she said. "That means 'you're welcome.' "

At lunch, Jessica, Giovanna, Lila, and Ellen met Jake in the sandwich line. Giovanna looked at the food and her eyes lit up. "I would like an American hot dog," she said. "With much mustard."

"Sure," Jake said. "My treat."

Giovanna looked at Ellen. "What does he mean, 'my treat'?"

"He means he'll pay for it," Ellen said.

Jessica smothered a smile when she saw the scowl on Lila's face. Jake had plenty of money, but she'd never seen him spend any on Lila. At that moment, somebody paused beside her. "Hi, Jessica," a boy's voice said.

Jessica looked up and caught her breath. It was Bruce Patman, the cutest boy in the seventh grade—in fact, in the whole school. Bruce almost never paid any attention to sixth-grade girls.

"Hi, Bruce," she said with her biggest smile. She glanced around to make sure that Lila and Ellen and Giovanna were watching. "How are you?"

"I'm fine," Bruce said, reaching for a sandwich. "How about you?"

Jessica tossed her hair back casually, but her heart was pounding. She and Bruce Patman were actually having a conversation! "I'm just fine," she said, her mind racing to think of something interesting to say. "Uh . . . I hear you've got a brand-new racing bike. How do you like it?" she said triumphantly, remembering something Aaron had mentioned.

"It's fantastic," Bruce said with a grin. He raised his voice. "It's an Italian bike. The best racing bikes in the world are made in Italy."

Giovanna turned around. "You have an Italian bike?" she asked. "No kid-ding?"

Some conversation! Jessica thought.

Jake handed Giovanna the hot dog she had ordered. "Here you are," he said. "A real American hot dog. How about finding a table where we can talk?"

"Yeah, the bike is awesome," Bruce continued, stepping in front of Jake. "After all, you can't win races if you don't have top-of-the-line equipment. Even if it does cost a fortune."

"In Italy," Giovanna remarked, "bicycle racing is one of our favorite sports."

Bruce started to say something, but Jake spoke up quickly. "I heard that Italians are really into auto racing," Jake said. "My uncle races cars. Occasionally I get to help him out in the pit."

Giovanna's eyes sparkled. "No kid-ding!" she exclaimed. "How cool! You must tell me about it."

Bruce pointed toward a table for two. "How about if we sit down, Giovanna?"

"We won't all fit at that table," Ellen objected. "How about that one in the corner?"

"Why don't you sit here, Giovanna," Bruce suggested, pulling out a chair. Quickly, Jake took the chair on the other side of her. Lila and Ellen were stuck across the table. Jessica had to settle for the end, but at least she was next to Bruce, where she could talk to him. And she knew exactly how she was going to get his attention.

"Hey, Bruce," Jessica said when they were all seated. "I want to invite you to the party Elizabeth and I are giving on Saturday."

"Party?" Bruce asked. "Who's invited?"

"What kind of party?" Jake asked.

"It's a pool party, so wear your swimsuits. We're inviting sixth, seventh, and eighth graders, too. We're going to have terrific food."

Bruce looked at Giovanna. "Are you going to be there?" he asked.

"Of course," Giovanna said. "The party is for me."

"I'll be there," Jake said.

"I think I can make it," Bruce said.

Giovanna smiled at Bruce. "Tell me about your American bike racing. It is very exciting, no?"

"Exciting and dangerous," Bruce said importantly. "One time I lost control coming down an unbelievably steep mountain. It was an incredible wipeout."

"Wipeout?" Giovanna asked.

"A big crash," Bruce said with satisfaction. "I'm lucky to be alive."

Giovanna gave him an impressed look. "No kid-ding," she said. "That is very awe-some."

Lila leaned forward. "Jake," she said, "there's something I've been meaning to tell you—"

"Auto racing is ten times more dangerous than bike racing," Jake argued. "Once when I rode with my uncle, another car bumped us at the far turn and sent us into the wall. We were pinned in the car and there was a huge fire. We were lucky that the fire crew got it out before we were burned."

"What an amazing story, Jake," Lila remarked sarcastically. "Why haven't you ever told it to us before?"

"I just didn't happen to think of it, I guess," Jake muttered.

Giovanna sat back with a sigh. "Such exciting things you Americans do. Me, I have only my little scooter. But it is fun to ride, especially on the hills around Florence."

"Your scooter?" Ellen asked. "You have a scooter?"

"That seems pretty unlikely, Giovanna," Lila said.

Giovanna looked straight at Lila. "You think I am not telling the truth, Lila? Perhaps you would like to see a picture of my scooter." She opened her bag and pulled out her wallet. "Here it is."

Jessica leaned forward to look at the photo of Giovanna sitting on a bright red scooter. Beside her was a good-looking boy astride a black scooter. Both were wearing chic leather jackets.

Ellen pointed to the boy. "Is that your boyfriend?"

"Your boyfriend, huh?" Lila said loudly with a triumphant glance at Jake. "He's very good-looking, Giovanna. I'll bet he misses you. I'll bet you miss him, too—a lot."

Giovanna laughed lightly. "That is my brother Alessandro," she said. "I have no boyfriend."

Jake smiled and pushed his chair back. "So, Giovanna, are you ready for your basketball lesson?"

"That is cool," Giovanna said, standing up.

"A basketball lesson, huh?" Bruce asked, getting up quickly. "Hey, Giovanna, I've got a great idea. How do you like tennis? I was thinking that we could knock a few balls across the net before the bell rings."

Giovanna clapped her hands. "Tennis!" she cried excitedly. "You play tennis, Bruce?"

Bruce grinned. "Sure," he said. "I played in the last city tournament."

"Did you win?" Lila asked sweetly. Everyone knew that Bruce had been beaten in his very first match.

"Come to think of it, I don't have my racket here," Bruce said to Giovanna. "Maybe we could get together for a game after school?"

"I play, too," Jake said quickly.

"Sorry. Tennis isn't a game for three," Bruce said.

Giovanna looked at Jessica. "Perhaps we could have a game of doubles," she suggested. "Do you play tennis, Jessica?"

"Sure," Jessica said. The truth was that she hadn't played very much. But she wasn't about to miss a chance to spend some time with Bruce on the tennis courts, where everyone would see them.

"Then it is a—how do you say?—a date?" Giovanna said happily. "We will knock the ball across the net, yes?"

"It's a date," Bruce and Jake echoed, scowling at each other.

Giovanna smiled. "I think it is time for the hoop lesson now," she said, getting up.

Jessica, Lila, and Ellen watched her walk off between the two boys.

Wednesday night, Elizabeth, Jessica, and Giovanna were helping Mrs. Wakefield clean up the kitchen after dinner.

"Well, Giovanna," Mrs. Wakefield said, "your first week of school at Sweet Valley is more than half over. What do you think of it so far?"

Giovanna put the last dish into the dishwasher. "The lessons are very easy for me," she said. "It is my English that is not so good. Elizabeth has been helping me when I have to write things."

"School is easy?" Mrs. Wakefield asked. "What do you mean?"

"In Italy," Giovanna explained, "we are ahead in math and science and languages. The work that you are doing here in math and science, I did last year. And everyone at my school has to take English classes, and French, too. Here, you do not have to take classes in Italian, and you do not start French until seventh grade."

Elizabeth sighed. Giovanna was right about being ahead in math and science. But Giovanna's English wasn't the best. In fact, the night before,

Elizabeth had spent three hours helping her with an essay for social studies class. But at least she could manage to make herself understood. Elizabeth knew only a few words of Italian, and almost no French.

"We do lots of things in school that you don't," Jessica said defensively. "We have the Boosters, for instance, and the class newspaper that Elizabeth works on, and band, and chorus. We get a free period for things like that."

Giovanna shook her head. "You are right, Jessica. In Italy, we do not spend school time on extracurricular activities. We have too much studying to do."

Mrs. Wakefield looked thoughtful. "Perhaps it balances out," she said. "In America, we think that working on a newspaper and playing a musical instrument are important ways of learning, too." She smiled. "Well, now that we're finished here, I have a little housework to do upstairs."

Giovanna made a face. "I must start *my* housework."

"I think you mean 'homework,' " Jessica said with a giggle.

Giovanna frowned. "Housework, homework—what is the difference?"

"Not too much," Jessica said. "Neither one is any fun."

Giovanna turned to Elizabeth. "Elizabeth, I must ask you to help me again tonight. There are fifty words on the vocabulary list Mr. Bowman gave me. And not one of these vocabularies do I know! Each one I will have to look for in the dictionary. It will take hours and hours."

"I'll be up in a minute," Elizabeth replied.

When Giovanna had gone, Jessica shook her head. "Well, her English might not be so great, but she sure doesn't have any trouble communicating with boys." She turned toward the door. "And she's a pro on the tennis court. She sure made Jake and Bruce look stupid this afternoon. Well, I guess I'll be going, Elizabeth. I have a bunch of homework and—"

"Not so fast, Jess," Elizabeth said. "Tonight's Wednesday night. You know what that means, don't you?"

Jessica rolled her eyes dramatically. "Are you kidding? Of *course* I know what that means. It means that I only have two more days before my science project is due, and I've barely started it. If I don't get to work right away, I'll be in big trouble."

"Jessica, today is *moving* day. Giovanna is moving in with you."

Jessica's eyes got big. "But Elizabeth," she wailed, "if Giovanna moves in with me tonight, I'll *never* get my science report finished! Mr. Seigel will give me an F on it, which means I'll fail the entire term! And if I bring home an F on my report card, Mom and Dad will *kill* me! You wouldn't want to be the cause of my death, would you?" she asked in a small, pitiful voice.

"Jessica—" Elizabeth began, "I—"

Jessica threw her arms around Elizabeth. "Elizabeth," she said happily, "you are the most excellent sister in the whole world."

"Jessica," Elizabeth said. "You know you're just stalling to keep from—"

"My science report is due on Friday," Jessica said quickly, "so Giovanna can move in that night for sure. OK?"

"But Jessica," Elizabeth said, "I really *have* to clean my room before the party, so people can use it if they want to change. Giovanna's things are everywhere, and there's hardly room to sit down. She keeps borrowing my stuff and losing it, like my hairbrush."

"I know, Elizabeth," Jessica said sympathetically. "You're so wonderful to put up with her for two extra nights. But I swear to you she can move in with me on Friday. You'll have plenty of time to clean your room on Saturday morning."

Elizabeth frowned. "That's a promise? Friday night and no later?"

"Cross my heart," Jessica said solemnly, "and hope to die."

"Elizabeth, are you coming? I need help with these vocabularies," Giovanna called from the top of the stairs.

Jessica gave Elizabeth a smile. "Thank you, Elizabeth," she said gratefully. "I knew I could count on you to save me."

Elizabeth heaved a huge sigh. "But who's going to save me?" she asked.

Seven

Elizabeth, Todd Wilkins, and Melissa McCormick were leaving science class on Friday afternoon when Mr. Seigel stopped them.

"Elizabeth," Mr. Seigel said, "would you mind dropping this note off in Ms. Wyler's room on your way out of the building?" He handed Elizabeth a sealed white envelope.

"I'd be glad to," Elizabeth said.

"Oh, and tell Ms. Wyler that the date has been set," Mr. Seigel added as Elizabeth started out the door after Todd and Melissa. "It's next Friday. Tell her that all the arrangements have been made."

"The date?" Melissa asked as they went down the hall. "What date? What is he talking about?"

She took the envelope out of Elizabeth's hand and looked at it. "Too bad it's sealed," she said. "Otherwise, we could—"

"Now, now, Melissa. That's none of your business," Elizabeth said with a laugh. "But don't worry. I have a feeling that by next Tuesday we'll know what it's all about."

"Next Tuesday?" Todd asked.

Elizabeth nodded. "Mr. Bowman told me today at lunch that Mr. Seigel and Ms. Wyler asked for a space on the front page of the next issue of the *Sixers*. They want to make an announcement."

"What are they announcing?" Melissa asked.

"I don't know," Elizabeth said with a shrug. "But it must be important. They wanted us to leave a big space. They're planning to bring in their information on Tuesday afternoon."

"Well, I guess I can wait until Tuesday," Melissa said. "Especially when there's your pool party tomorrow to look forward to. I've even bought a new swimsuit."

"Speaking of the party, how's the guest of honor doing?" Todd asked.

Elizabeth laughed. "It depends," she said. "She's doing great with the guys. She's got Jake

Hamilton to play basketball with, and Bruce Patman to play tennis with. And this afternoon at lunch, Winston Egbert promised to teach her some new Booster cheers."

"So what's the problem?" Todd asked.

"Giovanna's not doing so well with Jessica's friends," Elizabeth said. "Lila is jealous, and the others don't know what to make of her. She's still having trouble with English, too. It takes her forever to write anything."

Todd grinned at Elizabeth. "She's lucky that she's got such a good tutor."

"Thanks," Elizabeth replied. "But I'm about to quit. She moves in with Jessica tonight, and it'll be *her* turn to tutor."

"I thought she was going to move in with Jessica on Wednesday," Melissa remarked.

"So did I," Elizabeth said with a sigh. "But it's tonight, for sure. Jessica promised." She paused by the open door of Ms. Wyler's classroom. "Can you wait a sec? I need to drop this off."

Ms. Wyler was sitting at her desk just inside the door, grading papers. Elizabeth stepped into the room and held out the envelope. "Mr. Seigel asked me to give this to you," she said. "He said to tell you that the date has been set for Friday, and that all the arrangements have been made."

"Really?" Ms. Wyler's eyes lit up. "How wonderful! Everybody's going to be—" She stopped. "But I really can't talk about this until the formal announcement has been made, Elizabeth. I'm sure you understand."

"Of course," Elizabeth said, even though she had no idea what Ms. Wyler was talking about.

Ms. Wyler smiled. "We'll have the announcement ready to go into the *Sixers* on Tuesday. Then you'll know everything."

"How are your party plans coming?" Mrs. Wakefield asked the twins that night as they helped her prepare dinner. "Is everything organized?"

Jessica frowned a little. "Everything's organized," she said, "but I'm still a little worried about it."

"Worried?" Elizabeth asked. "What are you worried about? We've got everything we need." She began to tick off items on her fingers. "Hamburgers, hot dogs, buns, chips, dips, drinks, paper plates, napkins—"

"It's not the food I'm worried about," Jessica

said. "It's Giovanna. She's got all the guys twisted around her little finger. Lila and Ellen and some of the other Unicorns are getting kind of mad about it." She sighed. "I almost wish we hadn't planned to give a party for her."

Mrs. Wakefield smiled. "I'm sure it will turn out all right."

"I think it will, too," Elizabeth said. "I asked Maria to come over early and help us set up."

Jessica glanced at Elizabeth. "And Mandy's staying all night with me," she said casually. "She'll be here to help us get organized in the morning."

Elizabeth's eyes widened. "Mandy's staying with you tonight?"

"We have to clean up the yard," Jessica said earnestly, "and Mandy is willing to give us a hand." She turned to her mother. "Don't you agree that it's a good idea for Mandy to help, Mom?"

"The more help you have, the faster the work will go," Mrs. Wakefield said. She picked up a heavy casserole dish and went into the dining room.

"But Jessica," Elizabeth said, "tonight is the big switch. You haven't forgotten, have you?"

"The big switch?" Jessica asked with a puzzled frown.

"Tonight," Elizabeth said, "is the night Giovanna moves into your room."

Jessica put her hand to her mouth. "Elizabeth, I *totally* forgot about Giovanna," she said. "I'm so sorry! If there was any way I could move Giovanna in tonight, I would. But I just can't." She lifted her shoulders in a helpless shrug. "*Tomorrow* night, Elizabeth, after the party. I promise."

"But Jessica!"

"Elizabeth, you really *are* the most excellent sister in the whole, wide world."

Elizabeth sighed. "No I'm not. I'm just the most gullible."

"Hey, Jessica, this is a *great* party," Kimberly Haver said. She was wearing a bright green swimsuit. Sitting on the edge of the pool, she dangled her legs in the water.

Mary Wallace was sitting next to Kimberly. She nodded. "It looks like everybody's having a lot of fun," she said, "and the music is great." She looked around. "But where are the other Unicorns?"

"I don't know," Jessica said worriedly. "I was

about to ask you. Lila, Ellen, and Janet aren't here yet. And they're usually the first to arrive."

Belinda Layton swam up to them. "Hi," she said, hoisting herself onto the deck and reaching for her towel.

"Have you seen Lila, Ellen, and Janet yet?" Mary asked. She lathered some suntan lotion on her arms.

Belinda shook her head.

Kimberly laughed. "Maybe Janet wants to make a big entrance. When she heard that you were inviting Denny Jacobson—" She rolled her eyes dramatically. "Janet's *madly* in love with Denny these days."

Jessica sneaked a glance toward the other side of the pool, where Giovanna was sitting with a group of guys. Denny was there and, unfortunately, so was Aaron.

Belinda laughed. "Well, Janet had better hurry and get here, then," she said. "It looks to me like Denny's falling under Giovanna's spell, just like every single other guy at Sweet Valley Middle School."

Kimberly shook her head. "They all look so ridiculous gawking at her in that skimpy red bikini."

"It's no skimpier than yours is," Belinda said with a laugh.

"Maybe not," Kimberly said. "But she's got more to show off than I have." She turned to Jessica. "Jessica, inviting an exchange student was a good idea. But next time, would you please make sure that they send somebody who *doesn't* look like a fashion model?"

"Elizabeth, this food is really fantastic," Julie Porter said, helping herself to some potato salad.

"Yeah, Elizabeth," Maria Slater agreed. "It looks like you and Jessica slaved for hours to put all this together."

"We had plenty of help," Elizabeth said. "Mandy was here all morning, and Giovanna helped, too. With four of us, it didn't take too long."

Nora Mercandy walked over to the crowd. "So where *is* Giovanna?" she asked, pouring ketchup on her hot dog. "I haven't seen her in a while."

Julie nodded toward the other side of the pool. "She's over there," she said. "Surrounded by guys."

Nora laughed. "So *that's* why I didn't see

her," she said. "Denny, Jake, Aaron, and Bruce are all standing in the way!"

"I don't know how you could miss that fire-engine-red bikini of hers," Julie said with an envious sigh.

Maria giggled. "Yeah, you have to be careful if you stand beside Giovanna for more than about thirty seconds. She can give you an inferiority complex." She looked down at her yellow one-piece suit. "I used to actually like this bathing suit!"

Elizabeth laughed. "Hey, you guys, are we going to swim? Or are we going to spend the rest of the afternoon comparing ourselves to Giovanna?"

Maria licked her fingers and put down her plate. "Elizabeth's right," she said. "Let Giovanna *have* those guys if she wants them. I'm going to swim." She ran toward the pool. "Last one in is a wet geek!"

"Well, finally!" Kimberly exclaimed, as Jessica opened the front door for Lila, Ellen, and Janet Howell.

"We thought maybe you weren't coming," Mary said.

"Not coming?" Lila asked with a smile. "I spent all morning searching every shop in Sweet Valley for just the *perfect* swimsuit." She pulled off her red T-shirt and turned around proudly.

"Isn't it gorgeous?" Janet asked enviously. "I wanted to get one like it, too. But the saleslady told us it's one-of-a-kind."

"That's right," Ellen said. "Just wait until Jake sees it, Lila. He's going to love it."

Jessica stared at Lila's bikini, speechless. Lila was wearing the exact same swimsuit as Giovanna! "Jake loves it all right," Jessica finally managed to say.

Lila frowned as they made their way to the backyard. "What are you talking about, Jessica? He hasn't even seen me in it."

Kimberly pointed.

At that moment, Giovanna, Jake, Denny, and Aaron all ran laughing to the edge of the pool. Giovanna was the first to dive in. The three boys stood watching her perfect swan dive, then they dove in after her.

Lila's face turned as red as her swimsuit and she grabbed her T-shirt.

Janet gasped. "Is Giovanna flinging herself at Denny Jacobson?"

Mary cleared her throat and stood up. "Uh, excuse me, everybody. I think I'll get something to eat. I'm really hungry all of a sudden."

Kimberly jumped up. "I'll go with you, Mary," she said. "I'm starving." The two of them hurried off, leaving Jessica standing with Lila, Janet, and Ellen.

Janet stared at Jessica, her eyes narrowed. "Jessica," she said, "has Giovanna been flirting with Denny?"

Jessica tossed her head. "Why are you asking me?" she asked. "I haven't been keeping track of who Giovanna's been talking to."

"I was asking you," Janet said, "because Giovanna is *your* friend. *You* invited her here to Sweet Valley. *You're* responsible for what she does."

"Anyway," Lila said, "you *ought* to be watching her. That's *your* boyfriend she's flirting with, too." She pointed toward the pool.

Jessica and Janet looked where Lila was pointing. Giovanna, Jake, Denny, and Aaron were hitting a volleyball back and forth. Giovanna was laughing and splashing water, and every now and then one of the guys would grab her foot and pull her under.

"If you ask me," Janet said grimly, "that girl

is trying to steal *all* our boyfriends. I'm telling you, Jessica Wakefield," she continued quietly, "if you know what's good for you, you'll stay as far away from Giovanna Screti as possible. That girl is totally bad news."

"But I *can't* stay away from her," Jessica said. "She's supposed to move into my room tonight!"

"That bacon and cheese dip is really terrific," Amy Sutton told Giovanna. "You should try some."

"Bacon and cheese dip?" Giovanna smiled. "In Italy we do not eat junky food."

"That's *junk* food," Lila corrected. Lila had changed into a purple bikini of Jessica's and she was feeling better since she'd been able to pry Jake away from Giovanna for a few minutes.

Giovanna nodded. "The junk food, it is not good for the skin." She stroked her clear, blemish-free cheek.

Conscious of the tiny pimple she had noticed that morning on her forehead, Elizabeth changed the subject. "Melissa and I delivered a note to Ms. Wyler from Mr. Seigel yesterday," she said to Amy.

"You did?" Amy asked. She leaned forward. "Did you find out what their big secret is?"

"What big secret?" Giovanna asked.

"Mr. Seigel and Ms. Wyler have been acting really weird for the past couple of weeks," Amy told her. "They've been hanging out together and talking, and whenever anybody comes along, they shut up fast."

"But we'll find out their secret next week," Elizabeth added. "They're making an announcement in the *Sixers*. And there's some sort of important date coming up on Friday."

"I wonder what it's all about," Lila said.

Giovanna gave Lila an incredulous look. "You really do not know?" she asked.

Lila frowned. "Do you think you do?"

"Of course," Giovanna said loftily.

"What *does* it mean?" Amy demanded.

Giovanna laughed. "In Italy, when two people act as if they have a special secret, it can only be because they are in love."

Elizabeth's eyes opened wide. "In love?"

"In love?" Melissa said. "Are you serious, Giovanna?"

"I am serious, no kid-ding," Giovanna replied. "I am sure people fall in love in America, just as they do in Italy."

"Yes, but they're *teachers*," Lila said.

Melissa laughed. "Is there a law against teachers falling in love?"

"Of *course*!" Amy exclaimed, snapping her fingers. "Giovanna's right! Mr. Seigel and Ms. Wyler are in love!"

"So the announcement they're making on Tuesday—" Melissa began.

"—is their wedding announcement," Amy finished.

"And the date they've set for Friday—" Melissa went on.

"—is their wedding date!" Lila exclaimed.

"It must be so," Giovanna said wisely.

"I'm sure it is," Melissa said.

"After all, Giovanna, you're the world's expert on love," Lila said with a snide smile.

"I am not sure about that," Giovanna said modestly. "But in this case, I know what I say."

"This is fantastic," Amy said. "My two favorite teachers, getting married next Friday!"

Elizabeth looked at Amy. "I didn't know that they were your two favorite teachers."

"They are now," Amy replied with a sigh. "This is so romantic!"

Eight

"Ms. Wyler and Mr. Seigel—getting married!" Jessica exclaimed. "How fantastic!" It was only eight o'clock that evening, but Jessica had already put her pajamas on and climbed into bed when Elizabeth came in to tell her the news.

"Of course, it's only a guess," Elizabeth cautioned. "But Giovanna acts like she knows what she's talking about."

"I'm sure she does," Jessica said. "She certainly seems to know how to handle boys." She took out a tissue and blew her nose.

Elizabeth looked at Jessica. "Why are you in bed so early?"

"The party wore me out," Jessica said. "And I have a terrible cold." She sneezed.

Elizabeth folded her arms.

"Lizzie, I know what you're going to say." Jessica blew her nose again, more loudly this time. "I'll be glad to take Giovanna tonight. In fact, I'm looking forward to it. The problem is that this cold is really—"

Elizabeth narrowed her eyes. "If you think I'm going to let you get out of—"

"But I don't *want* to get out of it, Elizabeth," Jessica protested. "I'm just telling you about my cold. When I got out of the pool this afternoon, my nose started running. By the time everyone had gone, I'd developed a terrible cough." She coughed loudly to demonstrate. "You'd better not come any closer. I'm probably contagious."

Mrs. Wakefield knocked on the door and came in. "Jessica," she said, "Dad bought the cold medicine you asked for. How are you feeling?"

Jessica gave her a brave smile. "About the same," she said, and sneezed. "I just wish this cold would go away," she added. "I promised Elizabeth that Giovanna could move in with me tonight. But now I'm worried that she might catch my germs." She frowned. "Do you think I should wear a mask to protect her?"

"Jessica—" Elizabeth began.

"Maybe Giovanna should wear one, too," Jessica said. "For extra protection."

"I think," Mrs. Wakefield said firmly, "that Giovanna should sleep with Elizabeth one more night, until we see how you are." She turned to go.

"But Mom!" Elizabeth exclaimed. "Jessica has been making excuses for days! I *have* to get Giovanna out of my room! I can't stand another minute of—"

"Shh, Elizabeth," Jessica said. "Giovanna might hear you." She sneezed. "Listen, I feel so terrible about letting you down this way. You have every right to be angry."

Elizabeth took a deep breath. "OK. Giovanna sleeps in my room tonight, but *just* for tonight. Tomorrow night, after dessert at Mrs. Dalone's house, Giovanna is moving in here with you. Do you understand?"

Jessica smiled. "Yes, Elizabeth, I understand."

"One more thing, Jessica," Elizabeth said as she turned to go. "Do you *really* have a cold?"

Jessica blew her nose. "What do you think?"

"I think you get away with murder!"

* * *

"Is your cold better, Jessica?" Mandy asked at the Unicorn meeting the following afternoon at Lila's house. "Elizabeth said you were sick last night."

"That was last night," Jessica said. "I'm a lot better now." She had actually been preoccupied throughout the meeting, trying to come up with a new excuse for that night to keep Giovanna out of her room—and she knew it had better be a good one, or Elizabeth would never buy it.

"Isn't it amazing?" Ellen said, breaking into her thoughts. "About Mr. Seigel and Ms. Wyler getting married."

"Do you really think it's true?" Mary Wallace asked.

"Giovanna says so. And she's the expert," Mandy said.

"She *thinks* she is, anyway," Lila snapped.

"But it fits," Ellen said. "Mr. Seigel and Ms. Wyler have eaten together every day for a week."

"It makes perfect sense," Jessica agreed.

"Maybe we could do something for them," Mandy said.

"We could give them a party," Ellen suggested.

"You don't give parties for teachers," Lila said.

"We could get a card and have all the Unicorns sign it," Kimberly Haver suggested.

"We could all chip in and buy them a present," Jessica said.

"That's a good idea, Jessica," Janet said. "What kind of present did you have in mind?"

Jessica thought for a moment. "I'm not sure. Why don't we go to the mall tomorrow and see what they've got?"

Lila pulled out her purse. "OK. Let's start a collection for the gift right now. We can go to the mall after school tomorrow."

"Sounds great," Jessica said. She was always up for a trip to the mall.

"We can get a card, too, and have everyone sign it," Mary added.

"Let's meet at Casey's at three o'clock," Mandy suggested.

"Casey's? What are we going to get them, sundaes?" Janet demanded.

"The sundaes are for us," Mandy explained. "I can't shop on an empty stomach."

Jessica laughed. "Me, either."

"OK, OK," Janet said. "Casey's it is."

"This will be great," Lila said. "We'll give them the gift at lunch on Tuesday. In fact, we can have kind of a presentation ceremony in the cafeteria."

Mary nodded. "One of us can make a speech—"

"*I* can make a speech," Lila said sharply. "The ceremony was *my* idea."

Jessica shrugged. "It doesn't matter who makes the speech, Lila," she said. "All our names will be on the card. I'm sure it's something that Ms. Wyler and Mr. Seigel will remember for ever and ever."

Ellen took out her wallet. "It would be nice if Ms. Wyler remembers this at the end of the term, when she puts down my math grade!"

"Don't forget that Mrs. Dalone has invited us for dessert tonight," Elizabeth said to Giovanna as the Wakefields got up from the dinner table. "She's really excited to meet you." Elizabeth had been looking forward to the visit ever since Mrs. Dalone had called last week to ask her and Jessica to bring Giovanna over that night.

"You'll like her," Jessica said confidently. "She's Italian. Her parents came from Sicily."

"People from Sicily are more Sicilian than Italian," Giovanna said.

"Mrs. Dalone thinks of herself as Italian," Elizabeth said, remembering how happy she had been to show off her scrapbook and treat them to *spumoni*. "She's very proud of her Italian heritage."

"If she's proud of it," Giovanna asked, "she should pronounce her name right. It's Dalon*a*, not Dalone."

"I guess the Dalone family wanted to make their name sound American," Elizabeth said, beginning to feel annoyed.

"If you do not mind," Giovanna said, "I would like to work on my speech for Mr. Bowman's class until we are ready to go." She sighed. "I am so *nervous* about this speech."

"What speech is it, Giovanna?" Jessica asked.

"The one Mr. Bowman assigned me my first day. I am supposed to tell what I think about America," Giovanna replied. "I have the worry that I will not know what words to use. And I have the stage fright, too. I worry that people will laugh at me."

"No one will laugh at you," Elizabeth said. "Listen, we'll do the dishes and then come up to get you," she offered.

"Thank you," Giovanna said.

"Since you seem to have completely recovered from your cold," Elizabeth said to Jessica as she began to clear the table, "you must be all set to have Giovanna move into your room tonight, right?"

Jessica stacked up the dirty plates. "I *do* want her to move in," she said. "The trouble is—"

"Jessica," Elizabeth interrupted, "you've made your last excuse. You've turned in your science project, you don't have anybody sleeping over, and your cold is completely gone. Tonight's the night. You're not putting it off again!"

"You're right, Elizabeth," Jessica said quickly. "My cold *is* better. But as soon as we get back from Mrs. Dalone's, I have to learn a new cheer for Boosters. It's absolutely vital that—"

Elizabeth shook her head. "Learning a cheer is no problem," she said. "I'm sure Giovanna will be glad to help you. Winston Egbert has been teaching her all the new Booster cheers."

Jessica sighed. "It's not only that, Elizabeth," she said. With a grimace of pain, she clutched her back. "It's my back, you see. With all the cheerleading practice we've been having lately, my back is really, really sore. If I have to sleep on that hard cot, I won't be able to move in the morning."

"If you mention your sore back to Giovanna, she'll probably be willing to sleep on the cot and let you have the bed." Elizabeth picked up the dirty glasses and started for the kitchen. "And don't worry about straining your back moving the cot," she added. "Giovanna and I can help."

Jessica heaved a sigh and picked up the stack of plates. "Will you also help me wash my sheets?" she asked plaintively. "I'm all out of clean ones." She paused. "Of course, it's pretty late to start a load of laundry. Maybe we'd better wait and move tomorrow—"

Elizabeth turned around. "I'm sure we can find a clean sheet in the linen closet, Jess," she said firmly. "Tonight is definitely the night, and you can stop trying to weasel out of it."

"Who's trying to weasel out of it?" Jessica asked innocently. "I'm just trying to work out the details."

"So *you're* Giovanna!" Mrs. Dalone exclaimed happily, as the three girls sat down on the sofa in her tidy living room. "How wonderful to have you over! Now I'll get to practice my Italian." She leaned forward with a smile and spoke a long sentence in slow, halting Italian.

Giovanna turned to Elizabeth with a puzzled look. "What did she say?"

Elizabeth was startled. "Why are you asking me? *You're* the one who speaks Italian."

"That is true," Giovanna said. She shook her head. "But *this* Italian I do not understand."

Mrs. Dalone looked troubled. "I thought I was saying, 'It is a very great pleasure to have you as a guest in my house,' " she said. "It's a sentence I learned from my mother." Once again, she repeated the sentence in Italian. "Did I say it right that time?"

Giovanna shook her head. "No," she said, "you did not." Slowly, she said the sentence in Italian, emphasizing each word. "There," she said. "Now see if you can say it."

It took Mrs. Dalone two more tries to get it right. With each try, Mrs. Dalone's face looked more troubled, and Elizabeth felt more angry at Giovanna for being so rude.

Finally, Giovanna nodded. "That is close enough," she said. She turned to Elizabeth. "Mrs. Dalone's parents come from Sicily, from the south of Italy. Sicilians speak Italian differently. It is not pure Italian, as we speak it in Florence."

"My mother and father always thought it was pure Italian," Mrs. Dalone said quietly. "They were quite proud of their language. They spoke it at home even many years after they'd moved to America. I'll get your dessert, girls."

"Is there such a difference in the way Italians talk that they can't understand each other?" Jessica asked doubtfully.

Giovanna shrugged. "Is there not a difference between the way the people from the north and the people from the south speak in your country?" she asked. "Is it not sometimes difficult to understand people?"

"Sometimes we have trouble understanding," Elizabeth said, frowning. "But we don't say that one way of talking is more *pure* than another. It's all English."

Mrs. Dalone came back into the room with bowls of *spumoni* and a plate of small cakes. She managed a smile. "I thought you might enjoy these cakes, Giovanna," she said. "They're traditional Italian cakes, from a recipe handed down many generations in my family."

Giovanna leaned forward and poked a cake

with her finger. "I do not recognize them," she said. "Perhaps they could be Greek." She turned to Elizabeth. "Sicilian food is similar to Greek food," she said.

After that, Mrs. Dalone didn't say very much of anything. Feeling terribly awkward, Elizabeth finished her ice cream as quickly as possible and then hurried the others. "I'm afraid we've got to be going," she said, standing up to thank Mrs. Dalone for the dessert. "Giovanna is writing a speech, and Jessica and I have homework."

"So soon?" Mrs. Dalone asked politely. But as they left, Elizabeth knew Mrs. Dalone must have been very glad to see them go.

The minute they were safely on the sidewalk, Elizabeth turned to Giovanna. "Why did you say those terrible things?" she demanded.

"Did I say terrible things?" Giovanna asked. "I did not understand her Italian. I did not recognize her cakes. Should I have pretended?"

Elizabeth turned away without answering. She was much too angry. The only bright spot in an otherwise awful evening was the fact that at least she didn't have Giovanna sleeping in her room tonight!

Nine

"So how are things going with Giovanna, Jess?" Mandy asked, as the Unicorns sat around a table at Casey's after school on Monday, polishing off their hot-fudge sundaes.

"She finally moved into your room with you, didn't she?" Ellen asked.

"Yeah," Jessica said. "It's not going too well."

"What's the matter?" Belinda Layton asked.

"Put it this way," Jessica said. "I used to have to step over clothes to get to my bed. Now I have to *wade* through them. Giovanna makes *me* look neat." Jessica laughed. "I actually asked her to put her dirty towels in the hamper. *I* asked *her*. I suddenly felt as if Elizabeth had taken over my body. It was kind of scary."

The waitress brought the check, and the girls paid it and headed out into the mall.

"So did she do it?" Mary asked.

"Do what?" Jessica asked.

"Put her towels in the hamper."

"Of course not," Jessica replied.

Lila shook her head. "I don't see how you can stand having her in your house, let alone your room," she said forcefully. "I can't believe how obnoxious she is."

"She's not that bad," Mandy said, following Janet to the section of booths in the middle of the mall.

"Can she sleep in your room, then?" Jessica asked with a laugh.

"Mandy, she is that bad," Janet added. "She's a total flirt."

They all stopped to examine a booth where a woman was selling ceramic pots and vases with flowery designs on them.

Jessica picked up a vase. "This is kind of pretty."

"Are you kidding?" Lila whispered. "That is the cheapest-looking vase I've ever seen. We want to get them something *nice*."

Jessica turned around and scowled at Lila, then she turned back to the salesperson. "Excuse me, can you tell me how much this vase costs?"

"Uh, let's see. That one is two hundred and fifty dollars," the woman said.

They all walked away from the booth as quickly as they could so the woman wouldn't hear them laughing.

"OK, forget the vase," Jessica said. "It's way too cheap. Where should we try next?"

"How about Precious Stones?" Kimberly Haver suggested.

"We have to get a present both of them will like," Janet said. "Besides, we can't afford anything from there."

"How about the bookstore?" Mary suggested.

"If you were getting married, would you want a *book*?" Ellen demanded.

"How about Susie's Cards 'n' Stuff? They have really nice gifts," Tamara Chase said.

"Good idea," Jessica said.

Janet started walking in the direction of the card shop. "So did you guys see Giovanna throwing herself at Denny Jacobson today at lunch?" she asked.

"She wasn't throwing herself at Denny. She was throwing herself at Jake Hamilton," Lila argued.

"Come on, you guys," Mandy said. "She wasn't throwing herself at anybody."

"Yeah," Jessica said. "If anything, those guys were throwing themselves at her."

"Are you kidding, Jessica?" Janet almost shouted. "Are you blind? Do you happen to remember where *Aaron* was during lunch?"

Jessica shrugged. "At a table? Eating his lunch?"

"And whose eyes was he staring into?" Janet demanded.

"Oh, come on, Janet. So he was sitting with Giovanna. Big deal," Jessica said. "Listen, I know Aaron likes me, so I'm not going to get all nervous about this," she added confidently as they walked into the card shop. "It's not like he and Giovanna are going out on dates or anything."

"Hey, look at this," Mandy said, picking out a silver frame from a display in the front of the store.

"It's really nice. They could put a wedding picture in it," Mary said.

"It's perfect," Kimberly said. "How much?"

Mandy turned it over. "Um . . . thirty-two ninety-nine."

"Not bad," Jessica said. "We can afford it, can't we, Lila?"

"I guess so," Lila said. "Considering my generous donation."

They picked out a card and took their items to the counter.

"Could you gift wrap the frame?" Janet asked the salesperson. She pointed to one of the rolls of wrapping paper behind the counter. "We'd like that silvery stuff with the bells on it," she said.

"Yeah. And a silver ribbon," Lila added.

When the gift was wrapped and paid for, the Unicorns headed through the mall to the parking lot. As they were passing the frozen-yogurt stand in the middle of the mall, Janet stopped suddenly and pointed.

All the Unicorns stopped and stared.

There, sitting at a small table surrounded by shopping bags, were Aaron and Giovanna, gazing at each other over chocolate frozen yogurt.

"There they are," Jessica whispered the following day in the cafeteria. She pointed at Ms. Wyler and Mr. Seigel, who had their heads together over a corner lunch table. "Do you have the present, Lila?"

Lila held up the small package wrapped in silver paper. She looked around at the assembled Unicorns. "Has everyone signed the card?"

"I have," Ellen said happily, and the others nodded.

"Do you remember what to say?" Lila asked.

"When you give the signal, we're all supposed to shout, 'Congratulations on your wedding!' " Jessica replied.

Mandy giggled. "That ought to get a lot of attention."

"That's exactly what we want," Janet said with satisfaction. "This is excellent publicity for the Unicorns." She cleared her throat importantly. "Let's go."

Ms. Wyler and Mr. Seigel stopped talking and looked up as the Unicorns approached. "Hello, girls," Ms. Wyler said pleasantly. "What can we do for you?"

"Actually," Lila said with a smile, "we would like to do something for *you*. We know that you've been keeping a big secret from everybody. But now that we've found out, we wanted to be the first to congratulate you."

Mr. Seigel and Ms. Wyler exchanged puzzled looks. "But how did you find out?" Mr. Seigel asked, frowning. "We haven't announced anything yet."

Lila laughed. "It wasn't hard to guess," she said. She stepped forward and held out the silver-wrapped package and the signed card. "And now, on behalf of the Unicorn Club and its loyal members, we present you with this gift." She smiled. "You don't need to thank us," she added generously. "Your happiness is thanks enough."

"Isn't she laying it on pretty thick?" Mandy whispered to Jessica.

"Maybe," Jessica whispered back. "But it sounds great, doesn't it?" She looked around. Lots of kids had stopped eating. "Everybody's watching, too."

Mr. Seigel took the package that Lila handed him. "I really don't think—" he began.

"Thank-yous aren't necessary," Lila said grandly.

Ms. Wyler frowned. "But this looks like a *wedding* present," she said. "It's got wedding bells on it!"

"Of course," Lila replied with a smile. She turned and signaled to the Unicorns, who shouted at the top of their lungs, "Congratulations on your wedding!"

Ms. Wyler's eyes widened. "But we're not getting married!" Mr. Seigel and Ms. Wyler exclaimed in unison.

Lila's mouth dropped open. "You're not?"

"You broke your engagement?" Ellen asked woefully.

"There never was any engagement," Mr. Seigel said with a smile. "Whatever gave you that idea?"

"But . . . but you've . . . and . . ." Lila stammered, her face reddening. "And . . . and Giovanna said. . . ."

Her voice trailed off. In the silence, the girls heard a ripple of giggles sound through the cafeteria, growing louder as it went. Jessica felt like sinking through the floor.

Mr. Seigel smiled. "We might as well tell them, Ms. Wyler," he said. "We can't leave them in the dark any longer."

Ms. Wyler nodded. "Mr. Seigel and I have been planning a new science and math project."

"It's called SOAR!," Mr. Seigel said proudly. "That stands for Science Offers Awesome Rewards. It'll be announced in the *Sixers*. On Friday, a man from the national SOAR! project will be here to help us kick things off with an assembly. All the arrangements have been made."

Lila shifted from one foot to the other. "I . . . I see," she muttered. "Well, in that case . . ."

Mr. Seigel handed back the package. "You might want to return this gift," he suggested. "Under the circumstances, it probably isn't appropriate." He smiled. "Although Ms. Wyler and I thank you very much. It was nice of you to think of us."

"I've never been so utterly, so *totally* humiliated in all my life," Lila said a few minutes later, as the Unicorns were standing outside the cafeteria.

"I felt like a complete idiot," Ellen muttered.

Jessica bit her lip. "I felt like crawling under a table," she said.

"This whole thing," Janet said, narrowing her eyes, "is Giovanna Screti's fault. *She's* the one who started the rumor. It's time somebody taught that girl a lesson she won't forget—even after she's gone back to Italy."

Jessica nodded. Giovanna had embarrassed the Unicorns, hurt poor Mrs. Dalone's feelings, bragged about the glories of Italy until everybody was fed up, and had ice cream at Casey's with Aaron Dallas. "I totally agree," she said. "Giovanna needs a good lesson. And I think I know how to teach it to her."

Lila arrived at the Wakefield house that night after dinner. "Hi, Giovanna," she said cheerfully, as she came into Jessica's bedroom. "What are you doing?"

Giovanna threw down her pencil. "I have finally finished my speech for English class tomorrow," she said. "But I am not sure about my spelling. And some of the vocabularies—"

The phone rang. "I'll get it," Jessica said, and dashed out to the hall. In a minute she was back. "It's for you, Giovanna. It's Aaron Dallas."

Giovanna smiled. "Oh, yes, the cute one," she said, and hurried to the phone. When she came back, she said, "Aaron has asked me to throw the bowls with him. Do you mind, Jessica?"

"Throw the bowls?" Jessica asked. Then she laughed. "Oh, you mean, go bowling. Yeah, sure, Giovanna. Have fun."

"Jessica," Lila said, "maybe you and I could go over Giovanna's paper while she's at the bowling alley with Aaron. We could check her spelling and vocabulary words. It might help her get a better grade."

"What a good idea, Lila," Jessica said. "What do you think, Giovanna? Would you like us to give you a hand?"

"No kid-ding?" Giovanna looked surprised and grateful. "Giving a hand would be awe-some. *Grazie*."

"Don't mention it," Lila said with a little smile. "Just go on and have fun with Aaron and don't worry about a thing." Her smile broadened. "Not a thing."

By the time Giovanna got back from bowling an hour and a half later, Lila had already gone home.

"We had another idea," Jessica explained to Giovanna. "We thought Mr. Bowman would be more impressed with your paper if it were typed. So Lila took it home to type it on her typewriter. She'll give it to you before class tomorrow."

Giovanna frowned. "But I must have time to practice reading it," she objected.

"That's OK," Jessica said. "Because it's typed and double-spaced, it'll be very easy to read. Anyway, Lila will bring it early, so you can read it over before class." She grinned. "Hey, I'm hungry. Do you feel like making some popcorn?"

Giovanna nodded. "Yes, you are right, Jessica. Let us pop the corns."

Jessica laughed. "You have such a fantastic way with words, Giovanna."

Jessica and Giovanna were standing outside Mr. Bowman's room before English class the next morning.

"Where *is* Lila?" Giovanna asked frantically. "I *must* practice my paper before I read it, so I do not make mistakes in pronouncing my English. I want this speech to be perfect."

"Don't worry, she'll be here," Jessica promised, glancing at her watch and feeling almost as nervous as Giovanna. Last night, her idea had seemed so great. Now, she wasn't sure it was going to work.

Seconds before the bell, Lila ran up with an envelope.

"I'm sorry to be late," she said breathlessly. "Here's your paper, Giovanna, all typed."

"*Grazie*," Giovanna said, reaching for the envelope. "I am so nervous. I hope there is time to read it over before—"

The bell rang. "Uh-oh, time to go," Jessica said, nudging Giovanna into the classroom. "Don't worry. All you have to do is read the speech. You'll be fine."

When everybody was settled, Mr. Bowman smiled at the class. "Good morning," he said. "Today we're having a special presentation. Giovanna Screti will give us her impressions of our country."

As Giovanna went to the front of the room, Jessica squirmed in her seat and glanced at Lila. *So far, so good,* she thought.

Giovanna looked around nervously. "Please excuse me for having the flies in my stomach," she said. She frowned as Lila and Ellen giggled. "Have I made the joke?"

Mr. Bowman smiled. "We usually say 'butterflies,' not 'flies,' Giovanna," he said. "But I'm sure that Lila and Ellen understand. If they had to make a speech in Italian, they'd have butterflies in their stomachs, too."

Giovanna nodded. She opened the envelope and took out the typed pages. "My speech is called, 'How America and Italy Are Different,' " she announced, and began to read. Jessica leaned forward to listen.

"In my opinion," Giovanna read, "America is a wonderful country. There are many things about it that I have enjoyed. I admire the big buildings in Sweet Valley. I love American food, esp . . . especially the great party snacks, like potato chips, bacon and cheese dip, sodas, and—" She stopped with a confused look, staring down at the paper.

Jessica bit her lip.

Mr. Bowman gave an encouraging smile. "Go on, Giovanna," he said. "You're doing fine."

Giovanna frowned. "But I did not mean to say this," she said. "I mean to say—"

"I know you're nervous," Mr. Bowman said. "But don't worry about it."

Giovanna's frown darkened. "But I'm afraid that—"

"There's nothing to be afraid of, Giovanna," Lila said smoothly. "Nobody will laugh."

"That's right, Giovanna," Mr. Bowman said. "We're all on your side. Now, go ahead."

For a minute, Jessica was afraid that Giovanna would throw down the speech and stalk away. But instead, she began to read in a low voice, as fast as she could. By the end, after two pages of raving about American food, clothes, cars, and customs, she was racing through the words. Her face was beet-red, and she looked as if she were about to burst into tears.

When she finished, the class applauded. Mr. Bowman smiled. "I must say I'm a little surprised, Giovanna," he said. "I didn't expect you to pay America quite so many compliments. Isn't Italy better in *anything*? What about your delicious food? Your art masterpieces? Your world-famous architecture?"

Giovanna glared at Jessica. For a moment, Jessica held her breath. But Giovanna just shook her head and sat down without a word. For the rest of the period, she sat with her head bowed, not looking up. When the bell rang, she ran out of the room.

"Jessica," Lila said, "I have to congratulate you. That was a great idea."

"Really," Ellen giggled. "Did you see the look on her face when she got to the part about how American fashion is so far ahead of Italian?"

Out in the hall, Giovanna was waiting, her hands on her hips, her eyes blazing.

"You ruined my paper!" Giovanna cried. "You took out my words and put in yours instead!"

Ellen laughed. "You mean, you *don't* believe

that American junk food is the greatest in the world?" she asked. "Or that American cars are the best, and American buildings are the most wonderful?"

Giovanna stamped her foot. "You Americans!" she shouted. "You are so . . . so *locked-minded.*" She turned and walked away, fast.

"Locked-minded?" Lila giggled. "What in the world is a locked mind?"

Jessica frowned. "You don't suppose she meant 'closed-minded,' do you?" she asked.

Ellen sniffed. "If she meant 'closed,' " she asked, "why didn't she just say so?"

Ten

That afternoon after school, Elizabeth went into Jessica's room to look for her favorite blue blouse. She was startled to find Giovanna there. She was even more startled to see that Giovanna was packing!

"Giovanna!" she exclaimed. "What's wrong? Why are you packing your clothes?"

"I have asked Mr. Lane to send me back to Italy," Giovanna said. She folded her black leather pants into her suitcase. "Tomorrow morning."

"But . . . why?" Elizabeth asked.

"Ask Jessica," Giovanna said angrily. "She is the one who is responsible. She and that friend of hers, Lila. They put words into my mouth that

I did not wish to say. They made me look stupid in front of the whole English class."

"Hang on a minute, Giovanna," Elizabeth said, stomping out of the room.

Elizabeth found Jessica in the den, watching a game show on TV. Elizabeth marched in and turned it off. "Do you know what Giovanna is doing right now?" she demanded.

Jessica shrugged. "How should I know?" she asked.

Elizabeth grabbed Jessica's arm. "Upstairs," she said. "Right now!"

Upstairs, Elizabeth pushed the door open and pointed to Giovanna's suitcase. "I asked Giovanna why she was packing, Jessica, and she told me to ask you. So I'm asking. Why is Giovanna leaving?"

"Who knows?" Jessica asked with a shrug. "And who cares? After the way she's acted, maybe it's time for her to go home."

"The way *I* have acted?" Giovanna cried angrily. "You and Lila behaved badly. You changed my words. You made me say things I do not believe."

"Just what did you do, Jessica?" Elizabeth asked.

Jessica avoided Elizabeth's eyes. "We only changed a few words in her speech, that's all," she said. "We were sick of hearing her brag about Italy, so we put in a few good things about America."

"A *few*?" Giovanna said angrily. "You made it sound as if I do not care for my country! You made it sound as if I am not proud of being an Italian!"

"You tampered with Giovanna's speech?" Elizabeth asked. "Why?"

Jessica put her hands on her hips. "Because she started that stupid rumor about Mr. Seigel and Ms. Wyler," she said angrily. "The Unicorns were totally humiliated, so we paid her back by embarrassing her a little. What's so bad about that?" She scowled at Elizabeth. "Don't pretend that you weren't mad at her, too, after how mean she was to poor Mrs. Dalone on Sunday night. You have to admit you've been dying to get rid of her as soon as possible. All you wanted was to get her out of your hair."

"But I wasn't *in* your hair, Elizabeth," Giovanna said, hurt. "I was only in your bed." She threw another blouse into her suitcase and slammed it shut. "I think it is truly time for me to go back to Italy."

"No, wait, Giovanna," Elizabeth cried. "I didn't really want to get rid of you. I just wanted—"

She stopped and bit her lip.

"Yes?" Giovanna asked frostily. "What did you want?"

Elizabeth took a deep breath.

"Jessica's right," she said. "I was angry at you last night. I felt sorry for Mrs. Dalone, after the terrible way you insulted her."

Giovanna frowned. "I insulted her?" she asked.

"You insulted her Italian and her cakes, even though she had gone out of her way to be nice to you," Elizabeth said. "You really hurt her feelings."

"I did?" Giovanna asked, sounding surprised. "I did not realize." She shook her head. "Sometimes in English I do not say what I mean," she said. "Perhaps I should apologize to her before I leave." She glared at Elizabeth. "But I do not apologize to you. I do not like to be got rid of. I do not wish to stay in your hair."

Elizabeth thought back over the way things had happened. "It wasn't so much that I wanted to get rid of you," she said finally. "Jessica and I had each agreed to have you for half the time. I guess it was more that I wanted to make Jessica do what she had promised. I was sick and tired of hearing her excuses. But to tell the truth, Giovanna, I was also tired of my room looking like a hurricane hit it. I couldn't find any of my stuff, with yours piled all over everything. You borrowed things, too, and didn't give them back."

Giovanna sighed. "My mother is often angry at me for borrowing her jewelry," she said. "And the maid tells me I am not a neat person. These are things I know about myself."

"You have a maid?" Jessica asked, surprised.

Giovanna nodded. "I suppose that is why I do not have the good habit of hanging things up," she said sadly. "At home, someone else does it for me." She turned to Jessica. "But why did you invent excuses? Did you not want me in your hair either?"

"Well—" Jessica said. She stopped and thought. "I guess a lot of it was that I like giving Elizabeth a hard time." She glanced sideways at Elizabeth, laughing a little. "It's sort of like a game, coming up with different excuses. But another part of it was that I was mad at you for flirting with guys."

"I was flirting?" Giovanna asked. "Who did I flirt with?"

Jessica began to tick off names. "There was Jake and Bruce and Denny. And you went to the mall with Aaron, who is supposed to be *my* boyfriend. Lila and Janet didn't like it, either," she added. "They thought you were trying to steal their boyfriends, too."

"Steal their boyfriends?" Giovanna asked incredulously. "How would I do that?" She thumped her suitcase. "Put them in my baggage and take them back to Florence? And what would I do with them when I got them there? They do not speak Italian. And Jake is an awe-some tennis player."

"I think you mean awful," Jessica said.

"Just so," Giovanna said firmly. She wrinkled her nose. "He is so awful it is awe-some."

Elizabeth grinned. "You have to admit it, Jessica," she said. "Lila and Janet are just jealous. They don't like the attention Giovanna gets from Jake and Denny."

"Maybe so," Jessica said. "The truth is, Giovanna, you're awfully good at flirting. Lila and Janet and Ellen and I—we all envy you a little, I guess. We wish we could flirt as well as you do."

Giovanna threw up her hands. "But I do not

flirt," she protested. "I like basketball and bike racing and car racing and tennis and throwing the bowls. I like to tease and laugh and have fun. In Italy, if boys like these things, too, then we laugh and have fun, girls and boys together. Is it not so in America?"

"Sometimes," Jessica said. She narrowed her eyes. "But it wasn't just the flirting, Giovanna. It was also the bragging. We were all sick of hearing about Italy this, Italy that. And about all the great things you get to do in Italy—drinking coffee and wine, riding scooters. Here you are in America, and there isn't one thing you like about it."

Giovanna shook her head. "About America," she said, "I like very tall buildings and loud rock music and basketball. I like old blue jeans and hot dogs with mustard and soap operas on television and skateboards at the beach. And I like the Wakefield family and this nice house." She gave Jessica a serious look. "What do you like about Italy?"

"What do I like about Italy?" Jessica asked. "I like a lot of things. I like—" She frowned. "I like—"

"You see?" Giovanna said. "You have been so locked-minded about Italy that you cannot say one thing you like."

"That's not true," Jessica insisted. She glanced at Elizabeth, obviously stalling. "Is it, Elizabeth? Both of us like—"

Elizabeth tried to think of something to help Jessica out. "We like Puccini," she finally said.

"Puccini?" Giovanna asked blankly.

"Sure," Jessica said. "You know, *Madame Butterfly*. The opera."

Giovanna laughed. "Are you kid-ding, Jessica? Even *I* do not like Puccini, and I am Italian!"

Elizabeth laughed, too. "You know, Jessica, I have to admit that Giovanna is right," Elizabeth said thoughtfully. "We really were a bit closed-minded when it came to learning things about Italy."

Jessica frowned. "I guess maybe," she conceded. "But Giovanna was closed-minded, too. For instance, she wouldn't eat eggs for breakfast."

"If it is important for me to eat an egg for breakfast," Giovanna said solemnly, "I will eat an egg." She smiled. "I will even eat French bread."

"No kid-ding?" Jessica asked with a twinkle.

"No kid-ding," Giovanna said. She sighed. "Maybe I talk too much about the way things are in Italy because I am homesick," she said. "I miss my parents very much. I miss Florence. I miss Alessandro. I miss my scooter."

"I can understand that," Jessica said. "I'd miss my scooter, too, if I had one."

"And if I went away," Elizabeth said, "I'd probably bore people with lots of stories about Sweet Valley."

Jessica turned to Giovanna. "I guess I owe you an apology," she said. "For putting those things into your speech—and for yelling at you, too."

"I will accept the first apology," Giovanna said. "But not the second. I like it when you yell at me. I like it when Steven teases. It makes me feel as if I were back in Italy, where Alessandro and I are always fighting and teasing." She grinned at Elizabeth. "He is always inventing excuses to keep from doing what he promised, too."

Elizabeth grinned back. "At least a few things are the same in Italy and America," she said. She looked down at Giovanna's suitcase. "Giovanna," she said, "are you sure you don't want to stay? Now that we understand each other better, it seems kind of a shame to call it quits."

"Call it quits?" Giovanna asked, puzzled.

"But it was Mr. Lane I called," she said. "Who is this 'Quits'?"

"Calling it quits means to give up," Jessica said. "I agree with Elizabeth. I think you should stay."

Giovanna looked from one to the other. "You really do not want me to call it quits?" she said. "You really want me to stay, even if I am in your hair?"

"Yes," the twins said together.

"Whose room do I sleep in?" Giovanna asked.

Elizabeth paused. "You know what," she said. "I realize I've complained a lot, but I really wouldn't mind having you stay in my room again."

"Wait a minute," Jessica said. "You've already had her for four extra days. It's my turn."

Giovanna, Jessica, and Elizabeth stared at one another for a moment and then burst out laughing.

"OK, I'll stay," Giovanna decided. "But I must do two things right away."

"What's that?" Jessica asked.

"I must phone Mr. Lane and tell him I am not calling it quits. And I must visit Mrs. Dalone and tell her that I am very sorry for offending her."

Elizabeth glanced at her watch. "If we get a move on, we can do both those things before dinner," she said.

"Then let's go," Jessica said.

"Just one more thing," Giovanna said thoughtfully. She turned to Jessica. "You said before that I went to the mall with Aaron?"

"Yeah," Jessica answered. "I saw you there on Monday. So did my friends."

"This is true, we did go to the mall," Giovanna said. "But it was not because I wanted to steal your boyfriend."

Jessica looked up. "Well, why, then?"

Giovanna began rummaging around in her bags. "I wanted to buy presents for you and Elizabeth, to thank you for having me in your hair." She laughed and handed a box to Elizabeth. "Aaron said he would help," she added.

Elizabeth opened it. In it were two books: a big, beautiful one full of glossy color pictures of Florence, and an Italian-English dictionary. "Wow," Elizabeth said. "This is incredible. Thank you."

"For when you come to Florence," Giovanna

said, pointing to the dictionary. Then she handed Jessica a box.

Jessica opened it and pulled out a red bikini, just like the ones Giovanna and Lila had. Jessica started laughing. "Amazing," she said. "Aaron helped you pick this out?"

Giovanna nodded. "You like it?"

"I *love* it," Jessica said. "But Lila's gonna kill me!"

Jessica waited impatiently while Giovanna called Mr. Lane. "Well?" she asked when Giovanna came out of the den.

Giovanna was looking very puzzled. "He said that he is very happy to hear that we ironed things out," she said. "I told him that we do not do any ironing, but he just laughed. What does he mean, Jessica?"

Jessica grinned. "He meant that he was glad that we straightened out our problems," she said. "Are you ready to go to Mrs. Dalone's?"

"I guess," Giovanna said with a sigh.

A few minutes later, the girls arrived at Mrs. Dalone's house. The elderly lady answered their knock with a smile, but she looked a little surprised when she saw Giovanna.

Giovanna stepped forward. "I have come to apologize to you," she said earnestly. "I did not know how rude I was until Elizabeth and Jessica explained to me. I did not realize I was offending you. *Mi dispiace.*"

Mrs. Dalone's wrinkled face broke into a smile. "Thank you, Giovanna," she said. Her eyes twinkled. "Don't sweat it."

"What does *mi dispiace* mean?" Jessica asked.

"It means 'I'm sorry,' " Giovanna replied. "And what does it mean, not to sweat?"

The twins laughed. "That means, 'don't worry about a thing,' " Jessica said. "She accepts your apology."

"I will not sweat it," Giovanna promised Mrs. Dalone. "I will try to stay cool."

Mrs. Dalone laughed. "Perhaps the next time I see you, Giovanna," she said, "my Italian won't be as rusty as it was last night."

"Why?" Elizabeth asked.

"Because I am going to Italy!" Mrs. Dalone announced triumphantly. "I bought my plane ticket today. And I bought a set of Italian-language tapes. Before I go, I'm going to brush up on my Italian!"

Giovanna smiled. "When you come to

Florence," she said, "be sure to let me know. I want to show you our beautiful cathedrals and our museums, and take you to an Italian restaurant—" She caught Jessica's eye and grinned. "And of course we will find a place to eat hot dogs. With much mustard."

Jessica laughed as they said good-bye and turned to leave. "Now that that's settled," she said as they walked home, "there's only one thing bothering me."

"What's that?" Elizabeth asked.

Jessica sighed. "Giovanna, ever since you came, I've been dying to borrow that fantastic leather jacket of yours. Do you think maybe you could—"

"Of course," Giovanna replied promptly. "In Italy, I loan my clothes to my friends very often. But if you borrow my leather jacket, what will I wear?"

Jessica thought for a minute. "Would my denim jacket be OK?" she asked finally.

Elizabeth's mouth dropped open. "Are you kidding?" she asked. "I thought that was your most precious possession."

"It is," Jessica said. "How about it, Giovanna? Is it a fair trade?"

Giovanna grinned. "It is fantastic," she said. "In Italy, we think denim jackets are totally awesome!"

On Friday morning all the Sweet Valley Middle School students gathered in the auditorium for a special assembly.

"What is this assembly about?" Giovanna asked, sitting down between Jessica and Elizabeth.

"It's about SOAR!," Elizabeth said. "You know—the science program that Mr. Seigel and Ms. Wyler announced in the *Sixers* on Tuesday."

Jessica laughed. "You know, Giovanna. Mr. Seigel and Ms. Wyler's big secret?" she said teasingly.

Giovanna smiled ruefully. "Right. The big secret. But I think that my guess was a lot more exciting than this math and science program."

"I agree," Jessica said. "I'll take love over science any day."

"Science is for geeks," Lila agreed from her seat next to Jessica.

"Luckily for you, you'll be back in Italy before all this SOAR! stuff starts," Jessica said. "You'll be riding your scooter and flirting with cute Italian boys—"

"I do not flirt," Giovanna said, pretending to hit Jessica on the head with her notebook. She grinned. "I am just . . . friendly. Anyway, it's not so lucky for me. I will miss Sweet Valley."

"Sweet Valley will miss you," Jessica said. "Especially Bruce Patman—"

"Would you please be quiet?" Elizabeth broke in. "I want to find out about SOAR!. This program could be really interesting."

Both Giovanna and Jessica rolled their eyes. "Typical Elizabeth," Giovanna said.

Elizabeth laughed. "She's really starting to feel like one of the family."

"Anyway, Elizabeth," Jessica said. "This SOAR! thing sounds totally boring. Good thing I'm so horrible at science. I'll never get picked for the program."

***What will happen when SOAR! comes to Sweet Valley Middle School? Find out in Sweet Valley Twins and Friends #61,* JESSICA THE NERD.**

The most exciting stories ever in Sweet Valley history...

☐ **THE WAKEFIELDS OF SWEET VALLEY**
Sweet Valley Saga #1
$3.99/$4.99 in Canada 29278-1
Following the lives, loves and adventures of five generations of young women who were Elizabeth and Jessica's ancestors, The Wakefields of Sweet Valley begins in 1860 when Alice Larson, a 16-year-old Swedish girl, sails to America.

☐ **THE WAKEFIELD LEGACY: The Untold Story**
Sweet Valley Saga #2
$3.99/$4.99 In Canada 29794-5
Chronicling the lives of Jessica and Elizabeth's father's ancestors, The Wakefield Legacy begins with Lord Theodore who crosses the Atlantic and falls in love with Alice Larson.

Bantam Books, Dept SVT 9, 2451 South Wolf Road, Des Plaines, IL 60018
Please send me the items I have checked above. I am enclosing $____ (please add $2.50 to cover postage and handling). Send check or money order, no cash or C.O.D's please.

Mr/Mrs ______________________________

Address ______________________________

City/State ____________________ Zip __________

Please allow four to six weeks for delivery. SVT9 6/92
Prices and availability subject to change without notice.

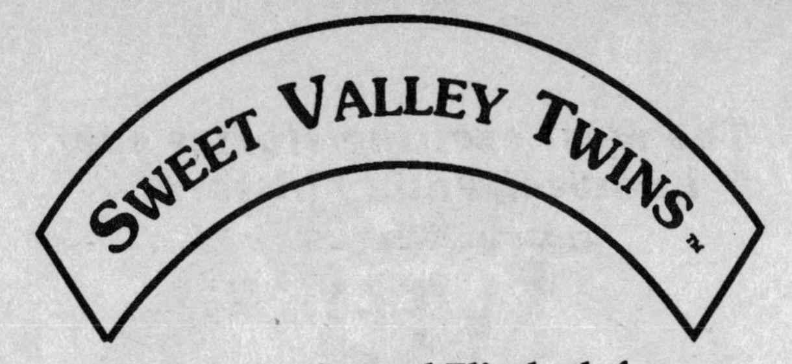

Join Jessica and Elizabeth for big adventure in exciting SWEET VALLEY TWINS SUPER EDITIONS and SWEET VALLEY TWINS CHILLERS.

- ☐ **#1: CLASS TRIP** 15588-1/$3.50
- ☐ **#2: HOLIDAY MISCHIEF** 15641-1/$3.50
- ☐ **#3: THE BIG CAMP SECRET** 15707-8/$3.50
- ☐ **#4: THE UNICORNS GO HAWAIIAN** 15948-8/$3.50
- ☐ **SWEET VALLEY TWINS SUPER SUMMER FUN BOOK by Laurie Pascal Wenk** 15816-3/$3.50

Elizabeth shares her favorite summer projects & Jessica gives you pointers on parties. Plus: fashion tips, space to record your favorite summer activities, quizzes, puzzles, a summer calendar, photo album, scrapbook, address book & more!

CHILLERS

- ☐ **#1: THE CHRISTMAS GHOST** 15767-1/$3.50
- ☐ **#2: THE GHOST IN THE GRAVEYARD** 15801-5/$3.50
- ☐ **#3: THE CARNIVAL GHOST** 15859-7/$2.95

Bantam Books, Dept. SVT6, 2451 S. Wolf Road, Des Plaines, IL 60018

Please send me the items I have checked above. I am enclosing $_____ (please add $2.50 to cover postage and handling). Send check or money order, no cash or C.O.D.s please.

Mr/Ms ____________________

Address ____________________

City/State __________ Zip __________

SVT6-2/92

Please allow four to six weeks for delivery.
Prices and availability subject to change without notice.

☐	27567-4	DOUBLE LOVE #1	$2.95
☐	27578-X	SECRETS #2	$2.99
☐	27669-7	PLAYING WITH FIRE #3	$2.99
☐	27493-7	POWER PLAY #4	$2.99
☐	27568-2	ALL NIGHT LONG #5	$2.99
☐	27741-3	DANGEROUS LOVE #6	$2.99
☐	27672-7	DEAR SISTER #7	$2.99
☐	27569-0	HEARTBREAKER #8	$2.99
☐	27878-9	RACING HEARTS #9	$2.99
☐	27668-9	WRONG KIND OF GIRL #10	$2.95
☐	27941-6	TOO GOOD TO BE TRUE #11	$2.99
☐	27755-3	WHEN LOVE DIES #12	$2.95
☐	27877-0	KIDNAPPED #13	$2.99
☐	27939-4	DECEPTIONS #14	$2.95
☐	27940-5	PROMISES #15	$3.25
☐	27431-7	RAGS TO RICHES #16	$2.95
☐	27931-9	LOVE LETTERS #17	$2.95
☐	27444-9	HEAD OVER HEELS #18	$2.95
☐	27589-5	SHOWDOWN #19	$2.95
☐	27454-6	CRASH LANDING! #20	$2.99
☐	27566-6	RUNAWAY #21	$2.99
☐	27952-1	TOO MUCH IN LOVE #22	$2.99
☐	27951-3	SAY GOODBYE #23	$2.99
☐	27492-9	MEMORIES #24	$2.99
☐	27944-0	NOWHERE TO RUN #25	$2.99
☐	27670-0	HOSTAGE #26	$2.95
☐	27885-1	LOVESTRUCK #27	$2.99
☐	28087-2	ALONE IN THE CROWD #28	$2.99

Buy them at your local bookstore or use this page to order.

Bantam Books, Dept. SVH, 2451 South Wolf Road, Des Plaines, IL 60018

Please send me the items I have checked above. I am enclosing $_____ (please add $2.50 to cover postage and handling). Send check or money order, no cash or C.O.D.s please.

Mr/Ms ____________________

Address ____________________

City/State ________________ Zip ________

SVH–3/92

Please allow four to six weeks for delivery.
Prices and availability subject to change without notice.